Published by: Swiyyah Productions Inc.

Printed and bound in the United States of America

Don't Call Me Crazy! Again

Again

SWIYYAH NADIRAH WOODARD

CHAPTER 1

Anika gapes out of her narrow window with her eyes stretched to her earlobes, looking through the morning dew in her small town called Saint Petersburg. She watches as a small bee lands on the window seal. Her heightened nostrils saturate the aroma of rubicund roses. Her eyes are glued to the window as she visions her wedding day. Anika imagines herself covered with a flawless snow dress joined by a six-foot train that flows out into an overturned bouquet of ivory roses covering her shoes. Mosi's inquisitive eyes question why Anika keeps speaking of David. Anika raised her wide-eyes to find Mosi observing her.

"You keep saying David. Where is David?" Mosi asked.

"He almost stopped our marriage," Anika said.

"Anika, are you ok?" Mosi questions Anika's bizarre behavior. She did not want to relinquish her visions. Mosi paces back and forth. The sweat from his bare feet moistens his eggshell carpet covered with the feel of rabbit fur.

"He caused you to hit your head on the pool," Anika responds as she gazes at mosi.

"No, Anika, you caused me to hit my head on the pool because you wouldn't give me the phone. Anika have you been taking your medication?"

"Sometimes," Anika responds.

"What do you mean sometimes? You have to take your medicine every day," Mosi said.

"Sometimes I have to wake up early for work. I can't always take my medicine," Anika said.

"Where is David, Anika?" Mosi asked.

"Why are you asking me weird questions?" Anika asked. Mosi ambles closer to Anika and places his hand on the top of her shoulder.

"Baby you have to talk to me," Mosi said.

"Didn't you confront David?" Anika questions.

"No Anika. The phone kept ringing and I heard static that day. I never heard David," Mosi replied.

"Didn't he almost stop our wedding?" Anika said.

"Anika, we're only engaged. We postponed our marriage until next year, remember?" Mosi said.

"I need to call Mary. She will explain everything." Mosi watches as Anika hastens over to the phone. He hits the floor with his eyes.

"Mary, Mosi's acting weird. He doesn't remember meeting David," Anika said.

"Yes, David; the one you're cheating on Mosi with," Mary said.

"We were both seeing David at the same time. Remember David was stalking us?" Anika said as she begins to pace the floor.

"Anika, I never meet David either. You said he was stalking us that day, but I never saw him. You need to take your meds," Mary said. Just as Mosi expected, Anika was losing her mind again. Mosi anxiously dials Anika's doctor. Anika signed papers to allow Mosi and her mother to know the details of her drug therapy. The doctor explained Anika had been delusional for months about David and her wedding day. He felt she was experiencing another relapse and needed to be brought into the emergency room. Mosi takes Anika by the hand.

"Anika I think I better take you to the hospital. Your doctor says David never existed, that you made him up," Mosi said. Anika had a chin of iron determination to get to the bottom of the truth.

"I didn't make him up. You saw a Caucasian man outside that day. Then he broke in and choked me," Anika said.

"Yes, I saw a man outside that day, but he never broke in, Anika. That was all in your head. Let me take you to the hospital. You're sick Anika you need help," Mosi said.

"I'm not sick. I don't need help." Mary enters the door and trips over her 3-inch heels exposing the dirt, which outlined her feet pattern.

Mosi gives Mary a look of disapproval and Mary puts her nose up in the air. She has a difficult time taking out Anika's medication from the pocket of her skintight jeans. Anika sits on the couch and Mosi places his two legs on top of hers while Mary tries to feed her the Abilify. To Anika the pills tasted like fried acid. Mary attempts to force the pills down Anika's throat with a glass of water and she causes Anika's lip to bust.

"I knew something was wrong with her. I should have known years ago. Hold her down harder; she might get away," Mary said.

"Anika you have to take your medicine," Mosi said. Anika jerks her head back and forth trying to miss the pressured pills. Anika looks up at Mary and Mary appears to her as a devil. Anika believes that too much medicine will kill her. Neither Mosi nor Mary knows how much medicine to give her. She is determined not to allow them to give her an overdose. To Anika, her refusing to take her meds is completely logical. Mosi punches his right fist into the couch and then picks her up into his chest and carries her to his car. Anika screams the whole time.

He sits her in the car while Mary watches from the back seat. The neighbors look on enjoying the dramatic scene. Anika taps the car window. The tap then turns into a knock, the knock gets harder until Anika slams her hand through the glass window cutting her skin to the bone. Mosi frantically takes off his white wife beater and hands it to Mary to cover the wound all while Anika lets out a piercing cry. "Ms. Sultan leave me alone!"

"Baby my mother is not here," Mosi said. Anika begins to hear voices in her head that sound like Mosi's controlling mother.

"I told you, you were too crazy for my son. Now look at this Mosi, she's gone nuts again and you want to marry her?"

"What should we do?! She's bleeding badly! I'm scared," Mary said.

Mosi's eyes stay glued to the road; his mind does him justice and blocks Anika's screams out.

"Didn't I tell you not to marry the girl? She's already causing you stress. She's not good enough for my son. You deserve someone like Mary. Why don't you marry Mary?"

Voices continue to enter Anika's head, taunting her.

"You should marry Mary. You should marry Mary."
Anika places her palms on the side of her head, hoping to
squeeze out the voices. *"You should marry Mary. You should
marry Mary."*

"You passed the hospital!" Mary screams.
"Mosi you passed the hospital!"
Mosi backs his car up without a three-point turn. He then
parks in front of the hospital. Mosi opens the door with his
left hand and drapes Anika across his broad shoulders and
carries her into the emergency room.
"We need a doctor! We need a doctor!" Mosi
screams.

The nurse announces the grief and doctors hurry to
the call. Anika struggles to stop the medication from touch-
ing her tongue. She fights for her sanity. The doctors warned
her about another attack. One more attack and she may
never be herself again. Was this it? A nurse practitioner runs
from behind the nurse's station, slips on a pool of blood, and
misses her shoulder and stabs Anika in the neck with the
needle. Her body falls upon the red garbage can; another
relapse.

Anika's body awakens to soft cotton sheets fitting her curvature. She turns three times on the twin size bed thanking God for this experience. To the right of her lays another bed. An African American young woman sits while manicuring her toes. On the dresser lays her beauty items. Each client gets soap, toilet paper, deodorant, feminine napkins, a towel and a washcloth. A curious inner voice cuts through her thoughts. There's a bathroom in her room, two beds, two dressers, and a newspaper at the foot of the door. This couldn't be a crisis unit. Patients are always treated as lunatics. This is not what Anika is used to. She's used to a stiff mat being her bed, standing in line for toilet paper, and an insane roommate keeping her up at night.

"Hi, my name is Tamara," Anika doesn't answer. She is sane and everyone else around her is delusional.

"I cleaned the bathroom for you and placed some feminine products on your side of the room. We even have feminine spray." Anika is really in shock.

"Who is this girl acting as if she's in a mansion? It's a crisis unit," Anika thinks. *"A place for the insane."*

"Med call, med call." Anika follows the voices. Something is quite different. The clients all have a carroty tint to their skin. Their hair has a look of malnutrition. Their teeth are rotten to the core. This isn't the same type of crisis unit that Anika is used to.

"Med call, med call. Everyone line up." Anika stands in line with the other clients. It's now her turn. She's handed Risperdal.

"Will I get the shakes? Medicine usually gives me the shakes," Anika said. Anika stares as the clients slowly take their medication.

"Twenty four hours in a day. What can I do with all this time?" Anika thinks. She is then called into the psychiatrist's office. He slightly throws her file so she could see.

"You have massive amounts of cocaine in your system." Anika looked as puzzled as ever.

"I don't do drugs," Anika said.

"Then someone has been slipping you cocaine," the psychiatrist said.

"Cocaine? Who could be slipping me cocaine? I mean my friends do marijuana, but I have never known them to do drugs." The doctor looks up from his notes. He notices there's a bit of peacefulness in Anika. There's something very spiritual about this woman.

"What religion are you?" the doctor asked.

"I'm a Muslim," Anika said.

"Maybe the drugs are the reason I broke down? Maybe I don't have a mental disorder? Is it true that a person on drugs can resemble a person with a mental illness?" Anika questions.

"But Anika you heard voices. That's a symptom of schizophrenia. You have to learn everything about your disorder, so you will learn what not to do," the psychiatrist said.

"When am I going to get out of this hell hole?" Anika asked.

"As soon as you get better," the doctor says.

"I hear voices. I need help," Anika said, keeping her eyes glued to her locomotive feet.

"What do the voices tell you to do? Do they tell you to kill yourself?" The psychiatrist asked while writing in a blank chart.

"Yes, they do. I need help," Anika said.

"Then it is fair to say that you are suicidal?" The psychiatrist asked. Anika could not answer at first for her paranoia caused her to not trust anyone in the medical field. She glared into the psychiatrist's eyes, hoping to read his mind, for she needed to eliminate any doubt that he would lock her up.

"No, sir. No, I am not suicidal," Anika said.

"When was your first suicide attempt?" The psychiatrist asked. Anika once more was silent. She was trying to figure out how this doctor knew of her suicide attempts. Who told him? She knew she did not reveal this information to Mosi, so it could not have been him to delude her. So who? Her mother, maybe, for her mother knew about the suicide attempts, but knew nothing of her voices. No one knew of her voices but her and Mosi. *"So who could the betrayer be?"* She thought to herself.

"My first attempt was when I was eight years old," Anika said.

"Did the voices tell you to kill yourself, then?" The psychiatrist asked. Anika could not deny the truth. She felt as if she lost in a mental chess game.

"Yes, they did," Anika said.

"So I am to assume that your voices tell you to commit suicide on a regular basis? Am I correct?" The Psychiatrist asked.

Anika again was without words. She had lost her second match in mental chest.

"Yes, they do, sir. My voices on a regular basis tell me to kill myself. They say that I am worthless to live, sir," Anika said.

"Then it is fair to say that you are suicidal?" The psychiatrist asked. Anika paused for one full minute this time. She wanted to make sure that this was not another trick question. How should she answer? She was unfamiliar with the Baker Act laws, so she was unsure how to answer. If she lies, then she will never receive the right treatment. If she is honest then that may give the psychiatrist a reason to lock her up. She thought back to her earlier conversation with Mosi. She remembers that he promised she would not be Baker Acted. He and her mother are the only ones she has ever trusted. Then she felt a warmth feeling of security come over her.

It did not matter how she answered for Mosi promised she would not be Baker Acted. Mosi waits for her in the security room. His knees can't stop shaking. It had been ten minutes now and Anika has not yet walked out with medication.

"Yes sir. You are correct I am suicidal," Anika answered.

"What happened when you were eight to cause you to want to commit suicide?" The doctor asked.

"My brother Rashid molested me. It started when I was five years old. I can't remember how long it went on for, maybe about 6 months. I didn't think anything of it. I didn't question it. I didn't know if it was wrong or right. I just knew it was happening. My mind didn't even tell me this was abnormal behavior and I didn't even try to stop it. Maybe I'm a little slow. Is it normal for a person to assume this was okay? My mom and step dad didn't even know this was going on. My mother caught him one day in my room on top of me with his clothes on. She told me to fight back the next time, so I did. I fought back and the abuse stopped. He didn't know what he was doing. When he was eight, he was molested by a little girl. My mom caught them. He tried to kill himself many times, until finally one day he was successful. There was something I should have told him, but I didn't. I didn't tell him he missed a call from his Imam who was going to give him a ride to go to Atlanta to sing."

"It wasn't your fault," the doctor said.

"What?" Anika responded.

"It wasn't your fault," the doctor said.

"Of course it was my fault. I didn't relay the message. And I should have never allowed him to molest me. I should have fought him off. I'm going to hell."

"Do you believe in Jesus? He died so you can have eternal life," The doctor said. Anika remains silent.

"Do you hallucinate visually or have delusions?" The doctor asked.

"Yes, I do see things that are not there, but I'm not really sure if I am delusional. I see faces everywhere, faces in my sheets, faces in the walls, faces in my rugs. Also, my husband always implies that I'm crazy because I tell him that I am special, that I was sent here to live for a reason. That it's my job to save the world," Anika said.

"Everyone's special. So how do you plan on saving the world?"
The psychiatrist asked as his eyes sticks to her medical chart.

"By letting people know that the world does not have to end as everyone expects it to. It is scheduled to happen, but it doesn't have to. We have brilliant minds and can save ourselves from wars, pollution, and future devastation. By informing others that there is a God and he loves us very much, I can save the world" Anika said. The Psychiatrist gives Anika a dead stare. Sullenness stretched throughout the room like a contagious virus. Anika's pupils shielded behind her eyelids.

"And David? Is he real to you?" the psychiatrist asked.

"Yes, I almost had sex with David. That would have messed up my whole life. I lay in the bed with him, but nothing happened. He fell in love with me and started stalking me. He almost messed up my wedding," Anika said.

The doctor places her chart on the table and looks into her eyes.

"Anika there never was a wedding and David is all in your mind. You never cheated on Mosi and he is not your husband he is your fiancé. I'm sorry to be the one to tell you this. You're delusional right now. You haven't been taking your medication so I'm going to have to Baker Act you, again. When released, if you come back we will have to commit you for several months."

"Please wait here," the psychiatrist said. Anika began to feel anxious.

The rhythm of her heart increases and her voices began to taunt her again.

"He is going to lock you up where you belong. And then he is going to kill you with a high dose of medication. You are finally doing things right. What an excellent way to die. Allow someone else to do what you are too chicken to do. Let someone else do your bidding."

Anika's feet fought to rise for she was frightened that her voices might be right. The psychiatrist planned to kill her. Anika begins to pace back and forth in the medical room. She then notices a camera above and walks closer to get a better view.

"You see how well planned your killing will be. It will be recorded for the entire world to see. Everyone wants you dead, including Rashid. He was a part of the plan all along. And you did not even suspect him. How foolish can you be?" Anika's lungs burst with flames of dread.

"No, No." Two orderlies dressed in hell black surge in and choke both of her arms. She felt as if they were taking her to the dark side. She put up a good brawl so they dragged her along the floor and into the seclusion room. She screamed for Mosi, but Mosi never came. He saw her on the security cameras, but was held down by three guards when he tried to come to her rescue. She awakens at 6 o'clock to four eggshell colored walls, which she found calming. The doctor moved her from the rooms with patients that were addicted to drugs to the rooms that were filled with patients that suffered from a mental disorder. The fluffy bed seemed to melt every part of her spine. The walls were immaculate with not a speck of dirt. There was a bathroom in her room that contained a shower and toilet along with clean, fresh towels and toiletries on the bathroom counter. She shared a room with another client whose bed was parallel to hers.

"Everyone wake up, it's time for your blood pressure to be checked," one of the mental health techs said. Anika stood at the end of the line. There must have been ten clients ahead of her.

"Med call, med call. Those who have had their blood pressure checked, please come to get your medication," the nurse announced. After getting her blood pressure checked Anika walks up to the nurse's station. The nurse hands Anika twenty-five milligrams of Abilify and a cup of water. Anika placed the pill underneath her tongue and drank the water. She then hurries back into her room and spits the pill out into the sink.

"I saw that!" Anika's roommate exclaimed. She was a petite thing with brunette hair appearing to have been cut with an ax, and freckles covering her cheeks.

"I'm Juliet. Let me introduce you to everyone." Juliet takes Anika by the hand as if she was a spirit guide and introduces her to the staff and patients. Anika felt love from everyone.

"These people actually care," Anika thought. The psychiatrist is a male in his forties with nicely combed hair and a small mustache.

CHAP T E R 2

"Group time! Everyone gather around please," the psychiatrist announced.

"I'd like to introduce myself for all of the new clients. I will be your psychiatrist for the duration of your stay. I don't think of myself as a doctor because I work for a living so you can feel free to call me Brian. I would like for each of you to introduce yourself and tell us your goal for today. Let's start with you," he points to Anika.

"My name is Anika and my goal for today is to get out of here," Anika said. The clients began to then giggle underneath their breaths. Everyone introduces themselves.

"My name is Juliet and my goal for today is to make my bed, take my meds, and like Anika, get out of here." A short young man stands. He brushes his straight hair to the side and off his face.

"My name is Leroy and my goal is to get back with my girlfriend. She left me when she found out I was crazy-"

"No, not crazy, mentally ill," Anika felt the need to interrupt.

"Well anyway six months ago I started losing my mind. It felt like I was going crazy and I was afraid I'd lose control. This would happen about two times a week. It all began one day when I didn't have my medicine. I thought to myself, what if I go crazy? And immediately after, in my mind, I started feeling like I would go crazy. I tried to talk myself out of it, but that didn't work. I would lie down to calm my nerves and my eyes would blink rapidly. Eventually I would fall asleep.

This kept happening every week and six months later, my worst nightmare came true. I lost my mind," Leroy said. "She doesn't want me no more because I'm crazy." Leroy swallowed hard and bit back his embarrassed tears.

"You have a chemical imbalance in your brain. It's your brain that has the problem," Anika said firmly.

"Yes, that's true Anika," Brian said. Everyone turns and looks at this scrawny young man screech his teeth.
"Some people are crazy they don't have a chemical imbalance. Like murderers and rapist," Peter said. For thirty seconds, no one says a word.

"My name is Janet and like Anika, I plan to get out of here today."

"My name is Peter and all my life I've been a normal person until my twenty- fifth birthday. I thought that someone in my house was after me so I started sleeping in my car. My girlfriend thought that was weird, so she called the police on me. And now I'm here. My goal is to be normal again," Peter said.

"Every day I want each of you to write down a new goal and the next day we will see if you have accomplished your goal," Brian said. After the group, most of the clients went back to their bedroom to sleep off the medication that had a sedative effect. Anika remained awake with Juliet.

"Can I ask why you're here?" Juliet asked. Anika did not want to answer, but since Juliet was so nice to her, she felt the need to give some type of answer, any answer that would shut Juliet up. "I'm suicidal," Anika said.

"Well then we have something in common. I almost drank myself to death. I'm an alcoholic," Juliet said.

"Are you an alcoholic, too?" Juliet asked.

"No, but I know my dad was." Anika said.

"Anika can I see you please," Brian said, holding the door to his office open. He looks down at her medical chart.

"You hear voices do you?" Brian asked.

"That is what my chart says doesn't it?" Anika said boldly.

"Please, I am only here to help you. I care about my clients. This is one of the best hospitals in the state of Florida. You will be well taken care of. Many people with mental illnesses are bright, so there's nothing to be ashamed of."
Brian presented Anika with a series of questions.

"How is the medication working for you? Does it make you drowsy? If you have any bad side effects that you can't live with, I can change your prescription. And when you take your medicine find out how long it takes to kick in, then you will know how long before bedtime to take your medication," Brian said. Anika knew she had to answer with a lie since she spewed out her medication earlier. She hates to lie, but if she didn't she would be forced to take the medication which she felt would kill her and her voices would win.

"The medication is working just fine. I have no side effects except feeling sleepy during the day," Anika said.

"Well, that's good. Are you hearing voices or seeing anything?" Brian asked. Anika had not heard her voices yet that morning so she thought saying, 'No,' would not be a lie. It would be the truth.

"No, sir, no voices, the medication is just great," Anika said.

"Liar, liar, pants on fire. We are still here. We haven't gone anywhere. We will be here until you finish yourself off or until the doctors kill you with medication." Other voices join in saying the same thing at the same time. *"Don't you remember when you first heard us? When you were a slut with Rashid. You turned a clean Muslim into a sinner. You should be ashamed of yourself. You should die. You're not worth living anymore. The verdict is in. You must die. You tried to slit your wrist in the car. We saw you. Why didn't you finish the job? We want you to finish the job. The world would be better off without you."* Brian notices her eyes expand with terror.

"Are you ok?" Brian asked. "Another lie," Anika thought to herself, "I have to tell another lie."

"I am fine. Everything is just fine. What's my diagnosis?" Anika asked.

"You don't know? The other doctor didn't tell you?" Brian asked with an obvious expression of bewilderment seen in his eyes.

"No, I don't know," Anika said. There was a ten second moment of silence.

"You have paranoid schizophrenia. No one ever told you?" Brian asked.

"No, really, what's my diagnosis?" *Anika pondered.*

"You have schizophrenia. I would not lie to you," Brian said.

"Didn't the doctor tell you? I had massive amounts of cocaine in my system. This is why I had a nervous breakdown. And when I had my first breakdown I had marijuana in my system. I'll admit my friends were smoking around me. I'm not schizophrenic and I don't need help!" With disbelief, Anika scurries out of the doctor's office.

"Breakfast time, everyone line up, please," one of the mental health techs said. Everyone stood in line and walked down to the breakfast area. The smell of eggs and bacon lingered past their noses. Anika was astounded. There was a choice of breakfast. A side of eggs with bacon or grits and sausage. Orange juice or tea. Muffins or a slice of bread. She tasted the sweet sugar in her strawberries she had chosen and then sits across from an older African American male.

"Look around, we're not like the others. We don't belong here," Andrew said, looking over his right shoulder. Anika smiles without saying any judgmental words.

"Why don't you call me sometime?" Andrew hands Anika a napkin with his home telephone number written in bold print.

"What do you do for a living?" Anika asked.

"I'm retired. I get $1800 a month," Andrew said. Anika thought that was enough to take care of her.

"So why are you here?" Anika questioned.

"Oh, a little depression. My son died and I'm having a hard time dealing with it," Andrew said.

"So why are you here?

"That's personal," Anika said. Anika takes the napkin and places it in her back pocket. Anika was slapped out of nowhere and a food fight broke out.

"Food fight, food fight!" The clients shouted. Eggs, grits, fruit, milk, sausage, soared across the room. Four techs charged in from smoking. The clients then shoved their food off their tables to hide the evidence of guilt.

"Smoke break. Everyone line up for a cigarette," one of the technicians said. Anika lined up with the rest of the clients even though she did not smoke. She wanted the opportunity to go outside to see if there were any possible escape routes. She sees an open barbed-wire fence thirty feet from where she stands. She begins to jog pretending she is running for exercise. She is almost there, almost to freedom when one of the techs spot her.

"Come back, please; no one is allowed near that gate," one of the mental health techs said.
The voices start to taunt her again.

"Ha ha, you dummy you thought you could escape. You're not smart enough. You're still alive aren't you? You should be dead by now. You're taking up space in the world. Why don't you do us all a favor and end it!" More voices join in.

"Ah ha, ah ha, you have schizophrenia. Ah ha, ah ha, you have schizophrenia." Anika places her hand up against her temples in an effort to shut out the voices.

"Fifteen minutes are up, everyone line up; we're going back inside," one of the mental health techs said. Anika hurries to the front of the line since she wants to be the first to use the phone. The phone then rings. Anika picks up the receiver to find Mosi on the other end.

"I'm not talking to you ever again. You betrayed me. Now they're going to kill me and it will be all your fault. I trusted you!" Anika's scolding voice cremated his ear lobes.

"Please, please, let me come and see you during visiting hours. I love you," Mosi said. Anika hangs up the phone and storms into her room and lunged onto her bed. Mosi finishes his sixth can of beer when Tony comes knocking on the door. Mosi wouldn't dare look in Tony's eyes as he shared his pain.

"Well, look at it this way, at least the bitch never cheated on you," Tony said as he pulls up his pants that advertises his white boxers. A quarter pound of weed falls from his pocket.

"Why you messing with this crazy girl anyway? I think you need a vacation," Tony said.

"I think she has a gift. She's not crazy. When she was hospitalized the first time she saw a ghost. And she knew without asking that the hospital was once a home of a woman that set it on fire. The ghost's dress was burned at the end. Anika found out later that all ghosts have a mark of death on their body. The mark is supposed to show you how they died," Mosi said. Tony begins to laugh.

"Come on man you don't believe this stuff do you? Come on. Let's get out of the burg. It's on me. Where do you want to go?" Tony asked. "We can go to Las Vegas," Mosi said.

"I noticed you've been drinking a lot lately. You may be becoming an alcoholic," Tony said.

"No man, not me," Mosi said.

"How often do you drink?" Tony asked.

"Man, every day, but what does that prove?" Mosi questioned.

"Do you drink in the morning?" Tony asked.

"Damn, yes I do," Mosi said.

"Do you drink to ease your pain?" Tony asked.

"All the time, that's how I can deal with Anika," Mosi said.

"Then my friend, you have a problem." They both begin laughing infectiously and Mosi sits his can of beer down onto the table.

"So what should I do, join alcoholics anonymous?" Mosi asked.

"Hey, we can go right now," Tony said.

"Alright man lets go," Mosi said and they clap their hands together. Mosi and Tony step into Mosi's Mercedes Benz to head over to AA. There are three women at the front of the door.

"Is this where we go for treatment?" Tony asked.

"Yes, we are about to start in a few," Kari the leader of the group said. There were Polaroid pictures on the wall showing those who have recovered from their treatment. Kari takes to the podium. She looks as if life has been sucked out of her.

"Hello everyone, my name is Kari and I'm an alcoholic. I wasn't always this way. I had a husband, a large family, and a good job. All that ended shortly after I took my first drink. At first I was a social drinker. I would drink at parties with my friends, but when I got home the drinking stopped. I didn't want to be a bad example to my teenagers.

"Well, one day my daughter went to a party with her friends and they decided to get drunk even though they were minors. I think her boyfriend is the one who got her drinking. She definitely didn't get it from me. She decided to drive drunk even though I taught her this was wrong to do. She ran a red light and smashed into a van, killing her and five other people. The van she hit turned over three times. Witnesses say she was driving about ninety miles per hour. This ripped me apart. I stopped wanting to go out to parties or hang out with friends. I just shut down. I stopped opening up to my husband. He got lonely and cheated on me so I kicked him out of the house. I started to drink to ease my pain, even though I knew you're not supposed to do that. When I would drink, I would get happy. All the pain in my life would go away. I would drink one can after another. I even started drinking in the morning and showing up to work drunk. My co-workers started talking behind my back and then the supervisor overheard them and called me into his office and told me he had to let me go. The excuse he used is that my work wasn't up to par. So here I am with a dead daughter, no husband, and no job. I would borrow money from my sister to pay rent until I heard her losing control and smashing something in her house. I pawned a few things until my house was practically empty. I had no money so I lost my house. And you know what? Somehow I always had money to buy alcohol. I ended up living on the streets. My husband took his children, but wouldn't take me in. I don't think I wanted to be with him anyway.

I started selling my body in order to save up enough money for rent somewhere, but you know every time I would save up the money someone would steal it from me. My sister felt sorry for me and moved me in with her and that's where I'm staying now. I work temporary jobs now. I've saved up five-hundred, so far. I met this young man at my sister's church and he invited me to these meetings and I would go every week. Finally, after six months I can now say I'm alcohol free. And you should be also," Kari said. Mosi gets enough courage to stand.

"My name is Mosi and I'm not sure if I'm an alcoholic," Mosi said.

"Until you acknowledge you have a problem, we won't be able to help you," Kari said. Mosi stands again.

"My name is Mosi and I'm an alcoholic." Kari smiles.

"I always drink with my boyz because I love my boyz. I never thought of myself as an alcoholic. I thought of myself as a social drinker. I would buy the beer and my friends would drink with me. I never drank when I had a problem until I met my girl, Anika. I thought she was cheating on me with David so I fought for the phone from her and I fell in the pool and hit my head. After that day something in me changed. I loved her, but fell out of love with her. She hurt me so bad that I had to do something to ease the pain so I drank. I drank until my eyes turned red and it worked; it eased the pain. Every time she would break up with me, I would drink. My friend Tony recently asked me if I drank in the morning and I said yes. That's when I realized that I had a problem. Before my girl Anika, I never drank in the morning. Now Anika is losing her mind again and I'm drinking more than I ever have. I need help," Mosi said.

"And help is what you're going to get. You came to the right place. I want you to sign up for counseling. You have to learn what you can do to ease the pain. You have to find a substitution," Kari said. Mosi and Tony drove to a corner store in their neighborhood and left the car running. A young girl walked up to him and asked him if he could buy orange juice for her baby. He bought the orange juice and the girl hurried along. After Mosi bought a beer, he and Tony walked out of the store to see that Mosi's car was stolen. Mosi throws his beer up against the wall. They walked for one hour to Tony's house and picked up two of his dad's rifles and truck. Mosi was on the passenger's side with his rifle hanging out of the window. They drove all around Saint Petersburg looking for Mosi's car. They were just about to give up and return to Tony's house when they saw Mosi's Mercedes. There were three teenage girls in the car. Tony hit the bumper of Mosi's car until the car slowed down. Mosi felt a bump underneath the car as if they ran over someone. The girls stopped the car and ran down the street. Tony saw two of the girls run, but didn't see the third. Tony busted one of the girls in the mouth and she fell to the ground.

CHAP T E R 3

Anika is bored. There's nothing to do. The television is available to watch, but the clients are only allowed to watch the news.

"Need something to do? Here, write in this," Juliet said as she throws a journal over to Anika. She begins to write:

"Dear diary. I'm in a hospital unit for the insane and there's nothing wrong with me. The nurses and doctors are trying to kill me. I want out. I'll do anything to escape this hellhole. Yes, I hear voices, but that's Rashid's fault since he molested me when I was young."

"Everyone line up. Time for current events," the counselor said dressed in a blue skirt that draped pass her bony knees. Anika stands holding an article in her hand. This star was being accused several times for child molestation.

"I chose this article to speak about because I feel that this artist is not guilty of these charges and those accusing him should be ashamed of themselves. He has done so much for the entire world. You can look into his eyes and tell his soul is pure. I love him," Anika said and then sits down and listens to the other clients speak about their current event.

"A mother fatally shoots two of her children. One girl and one boy," Juliet said.

"Oh you know she had a mental disorder," Peter said.

"Not necessarily. Many have killed others and didn't have a mental disorder. I know this because I have my BA degree in psychology," Anika said.

"Well, I think you have to have a mental disorder to kill someone. And God will punish her," Peter said.

"I agree with Anika just because she killed her two kids it doesn't mean she has a mental disorder. Some people are dark spirits. They breathe to do evil. They hate everybody and they've turned their backs on God. Remember, God never turns his back on us," Juliet said.

"One preacher told me I'm going to hell because I'm gay. I found a book on spirituality here at this hospital and it turned me around. Before the book I thought I was going to hell. I even tried to kill myself and ended up in here," Juliet said.

"If you're gay you should have succeeded. I knew you were gay when I first met you," Peter said.

"Well, Peter do you know what I've learned?" Anika questioned.

"Yeah, what's that?" Peter asked.

"I learned when you make a judgment call about someone you don't know you're really talking about yourself or someone very close to you," Anika said. Peter remains quiet.

"Group therapy, everyone line up for group therapy," one of the mental health techs said. The therapist stands in front of the chalkboard and draws a vertical line and then a horizontal line across the vertical line.

"Everyone knows this game; it's called hangman. I want you to choose a word related to mental health. Once the class guesses the answer, then I want you to explain why you chose that word," the therapist said. Anika gets excited and runs up to the board and grabs a small yellow chalk. Finally, something for her to do, that's a little fun. She draws twenty-two lines across the chalkboard. The clients raise their hands.

"Is there an A?" One of the clients asked. Anika then draws three A's on top of the small lines drawn.

"Is there a Z?" Another clients asked. Anika then shakes her head no and then draws a face.

"Is there a C?" Another client asked. Anika draws three C's on top of the small lines drawn.

"Chemical Imbalance," one of the clients yelled out.

"Can I ask why you chose that word?" The therapist asked.

"I chose those words because the words, 'mental illness,' should be stricken from the vocabulary and replaced with, 'physical, chemical imbalance,' because there is a chemical brain imbalance in clients who have mental disorders. And maybe that will rid some of the negative stereotypes associated with mental illness." Everyone looked up at Anika astonished that she could be so knowledgeable. Juliet walks up to the board and writes nine lines.

"Is there an A?" Anika asked.

"Yes," Juliet said and draws an A on top of one of the lines.

"Is there an E?"

"Yes."

"How about an H?"

"Yes."

"Homosexual," Peter said.

"Yes," Juliet said.

"So why did you choose that word?" The therapist asked.

31

"Because mental health professionals used to consider homosexuality to be a mental disorder. They've found out now that it's not a mental disorder. Some people are born that way. So I was born this way," Juliet said.

"I don't know about that. I have talked to a lot of people who are gay and they say they were molested when they were young." Anika said.

"Well, I'm gay and I was never molested. I started liking a girl when I was five years old," Juliet said.

"Do you know of any person in your family who was molested?" Anika asked.

"Yes, my sister was molested," Juliet said.

"You may not remember being molested. When I was working in the mental health field I saw a five year old boy molest his six month old baby brother," Anika said.

"Well, what about hermaphrodites? They have two different sexual organs. A man's part and female's part. How do you explain that? Did God make a mistake? Because I thought God don't make mistakes," Juliet said upset.

"I do know about hermaphrodites. Parents need to wait until the child becomes older and forms their identity before eliminating one of their sexual organs. Because only males can produce testicles with testosterone and only females can produce eggs and naturally form a womb for the eggs to develop in. So if you wait until they are older, you will know if they are male or female. Families have skeletons in their closet. I bet someone in your family knows what happened and is not telling," Anika said.

Juliet remains quiet while poking out her lips. Janet walks up to the board. She draws five lines.

"Is there a J?"

"No," Janet said and draws a face.

"Is there an A?"

"Yes."

"Is there a B?" Anika asked.

"Yes," Janet said.

"Abuse," Anika shouted out.

"So why did you choose this word Janet?" The counselor asked.

"I used to find myself getting involved with the same type of abusive men. My father was abusive to my mother so I think I look for my father in each man I date so I've learned to date someone I usually wouldn't date and every since I've tried that I've been successful. I learned that abusive men usually wait until you're vulnerable before they hit you. They wait until you're engaged or married, pregnant, or have a child with them. That way it won't be as easy to leave. One of the men I dated was verbally abusive. I left him because I saw the warning signs and then two months later he was arrested for strangling his girlfriend. You can learn a lot by being observant. Listen closely to the way a person speaks. Observe their body language," Janet said. After the group session, Anika walks back in her room, showers, and tries to sleep the rest of the boring day away. Anika lays in her bed and begins to shiver. The music box that sits next to the digital clock begins to sing by itself. It is 3:45 a.m. She's startled as she sees David sitting on the edge of her bed with his back turned to her and his head down.

"How did you get in here? I told you to stop doing that. You scared me." Anika whispers under her breath. David gently presses his index finger against Anika's lips to silence her. Anika bits down on his finger as he thrust it through her mouth. He then gently holds the bottom of her face and kisses her lips. He kisses her neck. Anika is overwhelmed by lust. David holds tight to Anika's underwear tugging to pull it downwards. Anika places her hands on top of his knuckles.

"I can't. I can't make love to you. You know I have someone," Anika said.

"He is not the right one for you," David said.

"You're not real. The doctors say you're not real. You're all in my mind," Anika said.

"You can see me can't you?" David asked.

"Yes," Anika replied.

"You can hear me can't you?"

"Yes," Anika said.

"Then I am real," David said. Anika takes her blanket and pulls it across her eyes. She peeks through a hole left in the blanket and sees that David has left.
Juliet stops shaking and looks over to Anika.

"He's a ghost. Didn't you notice how cold it got in here?" Juliet asked.

"You can see him?" Anika asked puzzled.

"Yes. He's a ghost. Tell him to go to God. He is dead. Tell him," Juliet said.

34

"How do you know he's a ghost?" Anika asked.

"I can see right through him. Isn't he transparent to you?" Juliet asked.

"No I see him as I see you," Anika said.

"Something traumatic must have happened to end his life. You must ask him what happened. He doesn't know he is dead. Don't you see that bullet hole in his shirt?" Juliet asked.

"I must call Mosi and tell him that David is a ghost. He must believe that I'm not crazy," Anika said.

Anika leaves the room to use the phone, but is unable to because an obese, dark haired young man is talking to his relatives. Ten minutes go by and the young man is still having a conversation.

"Excuse me, sir," Anika said.

"Hold on for a second. Don't you see I'm on the phone asshole?!" John said.

"It's been ten minutes I need to call my fiancé," Anika said.

"Go home asshole," John said.

Anika heads straight for him and seizes the phone from his uncompromising hands. John starts cursing at the top of his lungs and heads over to the nurse's station for some medication to pacify his nerves.

"Mosi I have something to tell you wake up," Anika said.

"It's four-o'clock in the morning Anika. What can be so important?" Mosi asked.

"I can prove to you I'm not crazy. My roommate saw David," Anika said.

"What do you mean she saw David? David is all in your mind," Mosi said.

"No Mosi, David is a ghost." Mosi was silent for five seconds.

"Now that is a possibility," Mosi said.

"I'm not crazy! I don't need to take medication," Anika said.

"Now Anika you have to take your medication for the rest of your life. You know you're schizophrenic and so is your father. Some people have the gift to see the unseen just as you do, but they don't have a mental disorder, but you do Anika," Mosi said.

"I'm going to find my father and prove to you that he's not schizophrenic either," Anika said.

"Your father and your grandmother are both schizo-phrenic Anika. Anika slams down the phone and marches indignantly from foot to foot back into her room.

"He didn't believe you, did he?" Juliet asked.

"Many of us mentally ill patients have the gift. The gift to see what others cannot see. Our minds move faster than everyone else. One day everyone will be able to see their deceased loved ones. You have to believe in the unseen. It's funny if you ask people if they believe in God, they will say yes, but ask them if they believe in ghosts or spirits they will say no. They can't see God, yet they believe in him. Why not believe there are spiritual beings besides God out there? You have to open your mind to the possibility," Juliet said.
Anika's voices find an opportunity to taunt her.

"Why did you tell Mosi? You should have known he wouldn't believe you. You're nuts. You're listening to us, aren't you? Normal people don't hear voices. Only crazy people hear voices. Why don't you just die? Do us all a favor. Stop wasting our time and do it." Other voices join in. *"Do it. Do it. Do it."*

"You're hearing voices again, aren't you?" Juliet says.

"How do you know?" Anika questions.

"I hear voices too." Juliet says.

"Do they tell you to kill yourself?" Anika questions.

"No. I hear my spirit guide talking to me. She's the one who told me you have schizophrenia," Juliet said.

"What's a spirit guide?" Anika questions.

"We all have a spirit guide watching over us. Spirit guides have lived before and they decided not to live again, but instead to come back as a spirit to watch over us. Does your gut tell you something is wrong to do or maybe something's telling you not to go someplace? Well, that's your spirit guide. I started hearing my spirit guide when I was only eight. I wasn't scared because my mother prepared me for it. My mother has the gift too. We're not crazy. You're not crazy and neither am I. Some of what you're experiencing is mental illness and some of it is spiritual. You hear voices because you're schizophrenic, but you see ghosts because you have the gift of sight," Juliet said.

"If you have the gift, then why do you take your medication?" Anika questions.

"I'm tired of having relapses. Aren't you? Isn't it embarrassing?" Juliet said.

"Yes, it is," Anika said.

"Some people can see spirits and ghosts and never have a relapse. The only time you need to take medication is if your mental illness is interfering with your work, home, or career. I can tell that the voices you hear are bothering you. Believe me those voices are not from God. You have a mental illness, Anika and you need to take your medication. The next time you have a relapse you may end up killing yourself or you could get into a car accident and kill someone. I don't want that on your conscious? Do you?" Juliet said.

"Once I was driving and something told me to slow down because someone is going to run the red light. So I started driving slow and would you believe it two seconds later someone ran the red light," Anika said.

"Yes, that was your spirit guide. We all have a choice when we pass to be reborn, to become a spirit guide, to become one with God, or to remain in heaven to learn. Some people have turned their backs on God or they don't know that they're dead and remain a ghost until an angel comes to free them. I've heard of people remaining a ghost for one hundred years until an angel came and freed them," Juliet said.

"Well, after I see all of my family in heaven, I'm going to become one with God. No way am I going to live this horrible life again," Anika said.

"Now you do understand you have to be an evolved soul of positive energy to become one with God. What are you doing to make sure you will be ready?" Juliet asked.

"I've learned from Psychology that in order to grow, you have to change yourself. I'm always looking for ways to improve myself. And I treat people with the utmost respect. We are all really one soul so if I hurt someone, then I'm really hurting myself," Anika said.

"You have to start taking your medication Anika. You can overcome your mental illness. Learn everything about schizophrenia. Learn about the common behavior of a person that has schizophrenia so you can do the opposite. If you have side effects from your medication don't stop taking it. It usually takes two weeks for some of the side effects to go away. If the side effects don't go away and they are still unbearable, you can always ask your doctor for something different. You have to find the right combination of medication to work for you. You also have to find someone who will listen to you without interruption, someone to ask questions to help you find the answers, not someone that forces their advice on you. You may need to hire a counselor." Anika and Juliet talk until the morning comes.

"Med call! Med call!" It's like clockwork. Med call, breakfast, visiting hours, smoke break, lunch, smoke break, dinner, snack, sleep, Anika has had enough. She wonders what her friends are doing. Rachel receives a call from Mary.

"That bitch is finally in the hospital where she belongs. She thinks she knows everything. She doesn't know anything. I've been slipping the bitch some cocaine on the sly. She never even knew."

"You mean to tell me you've been slipping Anika drugs? Why?" Rachel asked.

"She thinks she's perfect. She looks down on us because we use drugs. She doesn't deserve Mosi. She said she's been cheating on him with some guy named David. I think it's about time he finds out," Mary said.

"I think Mosi already knows," Rachel said. Mary leaves Rachel's apartment and heads over to Mosi's.

"What are you doing here? Anika's gone," Mosi said. "I think it's time we talked. Anika has been seeing another man. And I think it's about time you found out," Mary said.

"I know this already Mary. What are you trying to do?" Mosi questioned. "Anika doesn't deserve you. Look at me. What does she have that I don't have?" Mary asked. "She has my heart," Mosi said. Mary sits closer to Mosi.
"I think you should look at these," Mary said. She pulls down her shirt and her unrestrained breast falls out. Mosi jumps up from the couch.

"I think you need to put those back in!" Mosi said.

"Come on Mosi you know you've been wanting me since day one. I know you're no good. I saw that woman sitting on your lap that day at the club. I had to put you in your place," Mary said. "No Mary I'm not the one. I think you should leave." Mosi takes Mary by the arm and escorts her out of his apartment.

"Fine you son of a bitch! I know you're no good. You can't fool me!" Mary said.

CHAP T E R 4

"Visiting time," one of the nurses announced. Anika awakened realizing that she slept through lunch without anyone bothering to let her know. When she walks into the living room, she sees Mosi sitting down on the vinyl couch dying to see her once more; she then turns around immediately to head back to her room. Juliet grabs Anika's shoulders, pushing her in Mosi's direction and Anika complies. Mosi tenderly held her left hand. His fingers gently brushed away the hair from her face.

"What do you want trader?" Anika asked as her nostrils touch the ceiling.

"No, please don't think of me that way. I'm here for you no matter what happens. I had no idea the staff was going to lock you up in here. I am so sorry," Mosi said. Anika turns her back to Mosi. He then places lilac roses on her lap. Anika presses weight upon her feet to stand. Mosi locked his palms against her waist and places her on his lap. Juliet peeks out of the bedroom. The other clients turn and stare.

"I don't want you, please leave," Anika said. Mosi felt a blow to his heart. His chin sunk into his neck and his hands wrapped around his forehead.

"Leave please. Leave you don't care about me, you're ust as bad as Rashid!"

"Anika, what did Rashid do?" Anika says nothing.

"What did he do?" Mosi questions again.

"When I was young Rashid molested me," Anika said.

"Oh no. I'm so sorry Anika. What can I do for you?"

41

Anika turns and looks at Mosi with sad eyes.

"Nothing," Anika said. Mosi watches her walk away. Anika enters her room where Juliet was waiting for her.

"You know that man loves you. It's not his fault you're in here. You can't blame him you have to blame yourself. You have to take responsibility for your own actions," Juliet said. Before Anika went to bed, she asked God if there was such a thing as hell. She fell asleep and through her third eye, she began to have visions. God took her into the stars. She watches all the planets in our solar system pass by her. Then she wakens a little and remains in a lying position and the visions strengthen. She felt her feet, twisting rapidly through the solar system. She left the Milky Way galaxy and enters an unfamiliar galaxy. There's a brownish green planet in her third eye. She pauses in front of it and then enters the planet. There is a war going on. She sees gunfire and futuristic airplanes flying around. She thinks to herself, *"I can't believe I'm still awake and seeing these visions. God must see wars as hell."* A plane begins to head towards Anika and she becomes afraid and screams for her mother. Thirty seconds later she awakens fully and the phone rings. She walks into the dining room to answer it.

"Anika, I heard you scream. Are you alright?" Ms. Muhammad asked.

"How could you have heard me, Momma? You're thirty minutes away," Anika questioned.

"I'm very close to my children, Anika," Ms. Muhammad said.

The next morning Anika awakens. Before opening her eyes, she prays that she will be in her own apartment away from the hospital. It feels as if her world is falling down at her feet. She's afraid she may strip naked in front of everyone, and everyone will see that she's crazy. She refused to take medication, slipping it in her back pocket, or hiding it underneath her tongue. Mosi continued to see her each day. And each day when Anika saw Mosi she turned and headed back to her room. After spending a week in the hospital, she was a few days away from being released. Anika was awoken by a screechy voice. She looked throughout the room with eyes slightly shut and saw no one.

"Don't be alarmed. It is me. My name is Beth. I've lived before. I'm here now to help you. Continue to write. You will be well known." It was another voice inside her head, but this time it was different. It was a positive voice, a caring voice, not the horrific voices Anika grew up hearing. In her peripheral vision she sees an onyx shadow. Several onyx- hooded, yet transparent, four-footed entities glide from the shadow and stand before her. She begins to shriek and several techs dressed in magnolia coats race to her side. She put forth pressure against the air as her accelerated arms swung forcefully. The techs gently take her arms and escort her out of the room.

"They're coming for me! The entities from the dark side want me dead! They try to control my thoughts. They taunt me," Anika cries. Her knees are trembling as they fall onto the beaten floor. Amethyst supple wings that only she can see, shelter her in a haven of warmth. A syringe of Haldol is then pierced in her right shoulder. The next morning she awakens and sees Brian standing by her bedside.

"You have not been taking the medication that I prescribed? Am I correct in assuming so?" Brian asked. Anika does not say a word.

"You will not be released from this hospital until you are stable,"
Brian said. Anika turns her back. Brian then leaves her room.

"Dear Diary I want out of this hell hole called a hospital. I refuse to allow the doctors to kill me. I'm not taking any medication."

"Med call, med call," Anika steps to the end of the line as usual. When she drags her feet up to the window for medication, two nurses stand guard to ensure Anika takes medication. They will see her if she places the meds in her pocket and they will check underneath her tongue. She has to take the medication this time. By midday she feels like she is going to jump out of her skin. She can't stop moving. She paces back and forth in the living room. She washes three times a day. She reads every magazine in the hospital. She washes everyone's dirty clothing, just to rid the locomotive feeling. Anika stays in the hospital. The doctors wanted to make sure she did not try to commit suicide.

"Everyone get out your current events," Mrs. Foster said. Anika stands crying.

"My favorite singer died today. He has done so much for us. When I was sick, I was dancing like him. I always looked up to him. No one will ever be a greater performer," Anika said.

"How do you feel Anika?" Mrs. Foster asked.

"I feel sad and overwhelmed," Anika said. The nurse walks in.

"Anika, you have a phone call," the nurse said.

"Anika, I'm sorry to tell you this, but Mary has been slipping you cocaine," Rachel said.

"What? I don't believe you," Anika said.

"She's not your friend," Rachel said. Anika then starts to fall deeper into insanity.

"You have to forgive yourself for your sins so you can become one with God. And ask God for forgiveness. If you don't, you may be afraid to approach God. You may become a ghost. Some people choose to reincarnate to learn life lessons. People that do you wrong have to suffer more in the next life. It's karma! What goes around comes around. I didn't always have a 100 percent belief in God! And I know many feel the same way because people don't believe in what they can't see!
We all have to become more spiritual! One day we will all be able to see ghosts and spirits!"

"Anika, you have to be quiet or we will have to give you a shot," the nurse said. Anika screams louder.

"We all choose what obstacles we're going to face before we're born! We choose our mothers, our place of birth, the time we're born, our skin color, our children, our men, our enemies, and our friends! You don't have to be gay! You were molested," Anika commands.
"Anika, I'm warning you; you have to be quiet," the nurse said.

"Believe in God and the unseen!" The orderlies and nurses grab Anika's arm and gives her a shot of Haldol.

"You have to believe in the unseen! When you die you will say, "My God, I'm still alive…" Anika lands flat on her face.

45

CHAPTER 5

Mosi calls his mother, Ms. Sultan, and both her and his sister, Keshia take the first plane out to be by his side.

"She had a relapse again Mama. This might be the last time she can be herself," Mosi said.

"I told you she wasn't the right one for you. I knew the first day I saw her in the hospital. Now you know what you should do. You should leave her," Ms. Sultan said.

"Mama just listen! Mosi insisted. Sometimes, when people come to you with their problems they want you to just listen and ask questions. They don't always want you to solve their problems. Sometimes they need help to solve their own problems."

"Was she taking her medication?" Ms. Sultan asked.

"No," Mosi said.

"When did she stop?" Ms. Sultan asked.

"I don't know," Mosi said.

"Did you notice any weird behavior?" Ms. Sultan asked.

"She thought we got married. We're only engaged. She kept speaking about David," Mosi said.

"Is that the man she was cheating on you with?" Ms. Sultan asked.

"I don't think David exists. He's all in her head," Mosi said.

"Boy you really got a nut case on your hands," Keisha said.

"Don't call her that! She's not crazy. She's mentally ill and I love her." Mosi hears a knock at the door. Ms. Muhammad removes her lilac scarf from here natural ebony hair as she enters Mosi's door. Ms. Sultan looks her up and down while squeezing her nostrils.

"I came over here as fast as I could. They wouldn't let me see Anika. They only give us an hour of visiting time. That needs to be changed," Ms. Muhammad said.

"So this is Ms. Muhammad?" Ms. Sultan asked.

"Yes and who are you?" Ms. Muhammad asked.

"I'm Ms. Sultan."

"So you're the one who has been putting down my daughter," Ms. Muhammad said. All 360 pounds gather to stand a step closer to Ms. Muhammad.

"I've never told a lie on that girl. I've only said that she's nuts because that's what she is," Ms. Sultan says. "How dare you speak about my daughter in that way? You should be ashamed of yourself," Ms. Muhammad says.

"Well, if the girls crazy, the girls crazy," Ms. Sultan said.

"That's enough Mama. I didn't fly you down here so you can insult my fiancé. I think you should stay here while Keshia, Ms. Muhammad and I will go see Anika." The doctor shows the concern in his eyes as he enters the waiting room.

"Doctor, Anika said she saw a ghost. She said David is real. Is this possible?"

"There's no way to prove that ghosts exist, but Anika hears voices and she definitely has schizophrenia. You can always go and get a second opinion. I'm sorry to inform you, but I'm taking Anika into surgery. She has fluid in her lungs and her right lung as collapsed," Brian said.

At first glance Anika didn't recognize Mosi.

"Are you alright baby?" Mosi said.

"I'm fine. When am I getting out of here?" Anika questioned.

"You're not fine Anika. You have to stay longer. You have fluid in your lungs. The fluid caused your right lung to collapse. You're going into surgery this evening," Mosi said.

"Fluid in my lungs! Why do I have to go through this? Anika said.

"You've been clubbing a lot Anika. Maybe it's God's way of telling you, you need to slow down," Ms. Muhammad said.

"But how did I get fluid in my lungs?" Anika questioned.

"The doctors don't know. It could have been from a fall or the cocaine that was in your system," Mosi said.

"I thought you did not do drugs Anika?" Keisha said.

"It was Mary. She put cocaine in my water," Anika said.

"I can't believe her," Mosi said.

"Cocaine! Mary put cocaine in your water? I can't believe that!" Ms. Muhammad said. Three doctors walk into Anika's room.

"We have to perform a posterolateral thoracotomy and you will need a blood transfusion. Please sign these papers." The orderly pushes her to the operating room. The nurse places the epidural in Anika's back. Then she takes an alcohol wipe and wipes Anika's wrist and places the IV in her left arm and a feeding tube up her nose. As the anesthesia mask is placed over her nose, Anika slowly begins to sleep. "Scalpel please. I'm now making an incision in her back. We need to scrape her lungs. Rib spacers, please. I'm now scraping the lungs. She's losing too much blood; please more blood. She's flat lining! Code Blue!

"Scalpel please. I'm now making an incision in her back. We need to scrape her lungs. Rib spacers, please. I'm now scraping the lungs. She's losing too much blood; please more blood. She's flat lining! Code Blue! Defibrillator please." Five people rush in with a table. They hook pads to her chest.

"Clear!" Anika's body lifts up from the table.

"No good. Once more. Clear!"
'Thirty-eight grams lifts from her body. She floats straight up to the ceiling and observes her operation. She sees a white light. Her body is drawn to the light as if the light is a magnet. Her mind is playing tricks on her once again. Anika experiences a scene like no other. Her thirty-eight grams of weight elevates horizontal, without wings, to the field filled with the sweetish powdered sugar scented lilac roses. She's soaring above the frosted clouds over each continent. She flies by the unseen moon. She glides through the violet sky back to Earth landing in front of Gods Towers.

Her tearful family from earlier reincarnations waits
on the opal marble steps for her arrival. Inside the Towers, her
spirit guide and eighteen councilmen dressed in white jade floor
length robes are patiently waiting, with chart in hand, for her
welcome. They sit at a half oval magnolia marble table beauti-
fully carved and set in between two parallel moonstone ionic
suns dried columns.'

"You have a lot more work to do. You have to go back.
You're not following your destiny. Your goal is to save lives from
suicide. Please follow your spirit guide to the apse. He is waiting
for your arrival," councilman four said. Anika holds tightly to her
spirit guides right hand following her up the marble steps. The
door closes. Anika looks outside through the clerestory window and sees Him; a face without a body, a transparent energy
form void of color. He has a stern look on his face and opens his
mouth slightly.

"You're the one," A voice said.
Anika is not ready to go back yet. Her soul wants to explore.
She lands on top of a 30-foot mountain. She jumps from mountain to mountain, until she lands on the neck of a Brontosaurus.
She holds tight as he controls the ground. She slides down his
neck and onto a white unicorn. She leaps off the unicorns back
and rolls through the rose garden. The garden is endless and
smells of cherries. She observes the kids playing in the purple
garden. She flies above the unseen moon. She passes by each
of the planets in our solar system. She wants to go further. She
enters another galaxy. There are 12 planets, one sun, and two
crescent shaped moons. She enters one of the planets. She's
surprised that the people look like us.

They all form a circle and hold her hand to welcome her. She then floats to feel the water. The water is thicker on this planet than Earth. She could taste the salt water. The sea animals look similar to ours also. She passes through a shark's body. She then reaches the bottom of the sea. She goes down into the muddy dirt. There are several dead plants in the mud. Anika feels as if she needs to catch her breath. She then feels as if she is snapped backwards by a rubber band. She is now over her body again.

"I think she's coming back. Clear." She feels as if life has been sucked out of her.

"Tubes please. Now let's stitch her back up." Mosi, Keisha, and Ms. Muhammad are patiently waiting for the doctors to emerge with the news of how Anika faired.

"You can see her now," one of the doctors said. Anika wakens. There's an IV in her wrist, a tube up her nose, a catheter inside of her body, a tube down her throat and two tubes coming from her chest. Ms. Muhammad holds her hand as the nurse removes the tube from her throat. The two tubes in her lungs must remain until all the fluid has drained out. They remain for a month. When her mother comes to visit, Anika feels as if the sunshine has entered the room.

"Mama, I had a near death experience," Anika said.

"I know baby," Ms. Muhammad said.

"No you don't understand I flat lined," Anika said.

"I know baby, you almost died," Ms. Muhammad said.

"Mama, I saw God." Ms. Muhammad is quiet for a few seconds.

"Anika please don't tell anyone that. You will never get out of the psychiatric unit if you tell people that," Ms. Muhammad said.

"You don't believe me?" Anika said.

"No, honey. What you were seeing was an image of yourself. Do you know now that David is not real? He's all in your head baby. And the wedding never took place," Ms. Muhammad said.

"If you don't believe me how can I ever convince the doctors that I'm not mentally ill?" Anika questioned.

"Baby you're sick. You need help. You were doing well for a while on your medicine. You agreed that you needed help. Why did you change your mind?" Ms. Muhammad asked.

"You think I'm crazy Mama?" Tears began to blind her eyes.

"No baby, you're not crazy. You're the most normal child I have. You're just sick. Please promise me you'll take your medicine."

"Would you take the medication if it caused bad side effects? Anika questioned.

"What I would do is tell the doctors to give me different medication. I love living and I would do everything possible to save my life," Ms. Muhammad said. The orderly wheels Anika to the psychiatric unit. She takes the medicine each day and then regurgitates it. She is in her hospital bed when she realizes she still has the phone number from Andrew.

"I didn't think you would call me. I haven't seen you in a month," Andrew said.

"I was in surgery. My lung collapsed. I had a near death experience," Anika said.

"One time I left my body. I had an out of body experience," Andrew said.

"Do you take medication?" Anika questioned.

"They give me medication for bipolar disorder, but I don't have that. I lied and told them I heard voices. I'm getting a disability check for nine hundred-forty a month."

"I thought you were experiencing depression? And you told me you made eighteen hundred dollars a month. You lie too much," Anika said.

"I'm getting ten thousand dollars from social security. What do you want?" Andrew asked.

"A shopping spree would be nice," Anika said.

"How about I give you two-hundred dollars and you have sex with me?" Andrew questioned.

"No, I don't think so. I gotta go."

Mosi walks into the room and Anika rushes to put the phone down.

"You can go home now," Mosi said.

After one month of being held prisoner, she is free to leave. She has not forgiven Mosi. She doesn't want to see him, but she has no choice. This is the only way she is going to get out of what she calls a prison.

"I'm not talking to you. You can take me home, but I'm not talking to you," Anika said. Mosi drives her home and tries to hold her hand several times in the car but she shoves his hand away each time. He keeps his eyes on her while he is driving. He is afraid to say a word, afraid things will worsen if he speaks, so he remains quiet the entire trip. Before leaving the car Anika gives Mosi a long stare. He thought she would speak, but she doesn't say a word. Her elongated legs stretched for departure and stride callously. It takes his decelerated heart several moments before it could beat. He watches his woman walk away. He feels every step she takes away from him.

"What if I never see her again," Mosi thinks.

CHAP T E R 6

Anika waits for her mother to come home. She must find her father. Maybe he doesn't have schizophrenia? Maybe mental illness doesn't run in her family? Maybe her mother's wrong about her father?

On the way there she plays one of her favorite songs.

"The day is almost here when I will see you again. I'm missing you badly. I'm missing you badly."

Ms. Muhammad knows Anika wants to meet her father. How can she talk her out of seeing her father? This man almost killed her. She wants to protect Anika. When her mother enters Anika is preparing dinner for the both of them. Anika's nostrils soak up the smell of cornbread and fried chicken. Anika could feel the tension in the air. Does Ms. Muhammad already know what she wants?

"Mama, I need your help," Anika said.

"What is it, sweetheart?" Ms. Muhammad said.

"I need to find my dad," Anika said.

"Anika don't you remember that he shot me several times almost killing me. Don't you think this is a dangerous man?" Ms. Muhammad said.

"But Mama, I need to find him. Maybe you're wrong? Maybe he doesn't have schizophrenia? Most schizophrenics are not violent unless theirs drugs or alcohol abused," Anika said.

"He was an alcoholic Anika. I just don't think this is a good idea. He may still be on drugs," Ms. Muhammad said.

"Maybe it was the drugs that made him lose his mind? Maybe he's not schizophrenic. I gotta have hope right?" Anika said.

"He didn't always do drugs. He started beating me the minute we got married. He wasn't controlling when I first met him. He was very sweet. He started taking drugs a year after we were married. He started using cocaine. He would beat me over the smallest things, like not having dinner done when he came home, or because he thought I was checking out another man. He is a very dangerous man. I don't want him to hurt you Anika," Ms. Muhammad said.

"I won't let anything happen. If he acts strange, I'll leave right away. I promise you. Mama, what if I don't have schizophrenia? What if I'm normal? What if the drugs are the reason I got Baker acted? The medication will hurt me if I'm not really schizophrenic," Anika said.

"You are normal Anika. Go to the Saint Petersburg Islamic Center on Friday and speak with a man named Saleem. He knows where your father is located. He'll help you find him." Anika patiently waits for Friday. It had been months since she visited the house of worship so she is a little nervous to enter. She notices that she is short on gas so she pulls up to a gas pump to fill up her car. A car pulls up behind Anika. There's an elderly woman in the driver's seat blowing her horn and her forty-five year old daughter is sitting in the passenger seat. Anika first ignores the sound of the horn.

"Go to the other pump," Anika said. The elderly woman continues to blow her horn and this infuriates Anika.

"Take your ass to the other pump!" Anika screamed. The young woman gets out of the van and marches over to Anika with heavy feet.

"We wanted to use that pump! We were trying to fit our car in that space when you cut us off!" The young woman said.

"Leave me the fuck alone! I didn't cut you off. What are you talking about? There are several pumps you can go to. Take your ass over there!" Anika screamed.

"You bitch!" The young woman said.

"That shows what kind of person you are! Fuck you!" Anika said.

"Well, you cursed at me and my mother first so you're no better than me. You need Jesus," the young woman said.

"You're no saint yourself! Fuck you!" Anika screams. Anika has made it to the house of worship. It is humongous. The first thing you see is the lobby where people leave their shoes before entering the praying area that could fit about two-hundred people. The kitchen and restroom are in the back. The Imam begins to speak.

"You shouldn't live a life full of regrets. You shouldn't suffer over mistakes that you've made. We are all supposed to learn from our mistakes in order to grow. Read the Quran daily. Prophet Muhammad, peace be upon him, wrote the Quran for you, so that you could learn how to be a better person," Umar said. Umar holds up the Quran over his head.

"This is from Allah. This is the last scripture given to us by Allah. Muhammad is the last Prophet. There will be no more. When 911 happened the Qurans began to fly off the shelves. People wanted to know what was in the head of those Muslims, but listen to me clearly. Those Muslims were not following the Quran. Islam teaches peace. It's the only religion that could put an end to racism. Islam is the fastest growing religion. It teaches you not to curse, not to eat pork, not to drink. The Quran can save your life," Umar said. Anika raises her hand.

"How can I stop from cursing people out? I was just at a gas station and a young woman was bothering me so I cursed her out," Anika said.

"She was upset because you insulted her mother," Umar said.

"But how did you know her mother was there?" Anika questioned with a confused look on her face.

"God told me. When you get upset with someone, get quiet, if that doesn't work lay down, if that doesn't work, walk away. This is right here in the Quran." Umar said.
Anika stands and prepares for prayer with the other members of the place of worship. She wears a scarf, a buttoned shirt, and slacks. After prayer a young woman walks up to her.

"You're not dressed appropriately. The scarf should be around your neck and your pants should be all the way to your ankles," the young woman said. Anika puts up her five fingers to motion stop.

"I'm perfect in God's eyes," Anika said and the young woman walks away. Anika sees one of her old Muslim friends.

"Did you see how she approached me? Most people come in here to pray and as soon as they step out the doors they're clubbing, cheating on their husbands and eating pork. I don't want anyone to say anything to me. We are all sinners. Some people are on a physical level, they're worried about what people are wearing. Then you have people like myself who are on a spiritual level. They're concerned with becoming closer to God. They're not concerned with everyone else," Anika said.

"Yeah, you're right. I haven't seen you in a while. What have you been up to?" Ayah asked.

"I'm still trying to marry Mosi," Anika said.

"Oh, you still with him? Wow, how long has it been, eight years?" Ayah asked.

"More like nine years," Anika said.

"Nine years, and you're still not married?" Ayah said.

"We'll you know what? Two years after we dated, Mosi sent me a letter asking me to marry him. Before I got the letter he called me and asked me what I thought about marriage and me being stupid I said it was too soon. I didn't know he was serious and then I got the letter. Man, where would we be if I would have only said yes?" Anika said.

"Doesn't he cheat on you though?" Ayah asked.

"I don't know for sure, but I don't think so. Enough of that, what have you been up to?" Anika asked.

"Trying to stay out of trouble. I got arrested for trying to cash bad checks. They gave me six months of probation. I want to do right for my daughter. Will you to pray for me," Ayah said.

"I can't do that. You have to pray for yourself. What's so hard about doing the right thing? You're not starving. You have a place to stay. Why can't you do right? I don't understand. You just don't hurt people," Anika said.

"It's not that easy. I feel bad that I can't do for my daughter. I want to make it. I can't find a job because of my police record. Nobody wants to hire me so what am I supposed to do?" Ayah said.

"Well, imagine yourself in jail. Who would take care of your daughter? She would be lost. If you can't stop for Allah, stop for your daughter," Anika said.

"I hear you," Ayah said. Anika sees Saleem is sitting next to the other men in the house of worship. She's a little nervous to approach him, but she does.

"Saleem I need to talk to you about my father. I need to find him," Anika said.

"You can find him in Virginia. Call Brother Aimer and he will take you to him. Here is his number," Saleem said. Anika is excited, but she has no one with whom to share the good news. She's still upset with Mosi. Anika then receives a call from Rachel.

"I think you need to come over to this party on East Bay; I'll text you the address. Mary is here, you can finally confront her," Rachel said.

"Oh, I'm coming right over there and I will confront her!" Anika said. Anika thinks she sees Mosi sitting on the couch next to Mary. Anika pushes through the crowd of people, but loses sight of the man that looks like Mosi.

She enters the back room and then sees the back door wide open. The man has left. Without warning Anika moves with long purposeful strides toward Mary and grips her by the arm. Anika felt her fists bunching at her side. Mary snatches her arm away and stands up abruptly.

"What's going on between you two?!" Anika presses her lips together in anger.

"Who told you? Rachel?" Mary said. Anika pushes air until her palm lands on Mary's face.

"You know I'm engaged to Mosi, and you're giving me cocaine! How could you do that?" Anika said.

"Let me explain!" Mary said. Anika turns away not waiting for an answer and heads for the door.

CHAP T E R 7

Anika ambles into her room and sees David sitting on the edge of her bed.

"What are you doing here?" Anika questions.

"Waiting for you," David said.

"David I have something to tell you," Anika said.

"You're going to tell me how much you love me." David said.

"David you're dead," Anika said. A white light appears in front of David. David feels as if a force is tugging at his waist side. His eyes seem to stretch widely.

"David you must go to God," Anika said.

"That's not true. It couldn't be true," David said.

"I never noticed before, but you always wear the same thing. Every day, it's the same thing. And there's a bullet hole in your shirt. David you've been shot," Anika said.

"Yes, I was shot," David said.

"You never went to the hospital, did you?" Anika questions.

"No, I never went to the hospital," David said.

"You need to go to the light David. Go to God," Anika said.

"But I've sinned. God wouldn't forgive me." The white light gets dimmer.

"You're a liar! I'm not dead!" David bawls. David takes Anika by the arm and slams her up against the wall. Blood is leaving her forehead. Anika is caught off guard by the sudden vibrancy of his voice. Ms. Muhammad comes flying in. She sees Anika bounce off the walls. She thinks she's trying to kill herself.

"Anika what are you doing?" A flicker of apprehension coursed through her.

"Can you see him? Can you see David?" Anika screams. Ms. Muhammad holds Anika in her arms and walks her over to the bathroom to wipe the blood.

"David does not exist Anika." Ms. Muhammad said.

"He's all in your head baby," Ms. Muhammad said.

"He's a ghost Mama and he doesn't believe that he's dead. Please don't call the police on me. I'm not trying to kill myself," Anika said.

"I believe you Anika. I believe you," Ms. Muhammad said. David stands before the light. A thirty-year old woman walks up to David and takes David by the hand and leads him to the light.

"Will God forgive me? I don't want to go to hell," David said.

"You have been saved. Ask God for forgiveness. You must come with me," the spirit guide said. Anika watches as the light gets dimmer and fades away.

"David is gone Mama. He's gone," Anika said. Ms. Muhammad embraces Anika and combs her hair to relax her. Anika falls asleep in her arms.

The next day Anika visit's the pier. This is where she and Mosi had their first date. This is where she feels the safest. Anika takes the elevator to the fifth floor, and as she exists she sees Mosi walking towards her.

"Baby, I missed you," Mosi said. Anika hides her face in his muscles.

"You were cute back then now you're beautiful," Mosi said.

"That's right. I may be almost thirty, but I still got it," Anika said.

"Yes, you do. I can't believe you're going to be my wife in a few more months," Mosi said.

"Yeah, me and Mary have to start planning for my big day," Anika said.

"Mary?" Mosi questions.

"Yes, Mary. She's my best friend. Who else would I have as my maid of honor?" Anika said.

"What about-"

"What about what?" Anika said.

"She tried to come on to me," Mosi said.

"I suspected that, but I have to forgive her. Forgiving is for me not her. When I forgive all the pain of what she did goes away," Anika said.

"But she tried twice," Mosi said.

"When?" Anika asked.

"When you left your mother's house for your walk," Mosi said.

"No, I don't believe that," Anika said.

"Believe it. Forgiving is good, but you should never forget. Just because you forgive a person, it doesn't mean you have to be around them. Don't allow her to make the same mistake," Mosi said.

"You don't like her do you?" Anika said.

"No, I don't. She's not your friend," Mosi said.

"How about you, don't tell me who my friends are and I won't keep you from your women hating friends," Anika said.

"I love my boys. What are you to trying to say?" Mosi asked.

"I'm not trying to say anything; I'm calling them haters. That's what I'm saying. They will never be faithful to a woman," Anika said.

"They're my friends, so do you think I'm unfaithful? I've never cheated on you," Mosi said.

"I don't believe you," Anika said.

CHAP T E R 8

Anika calls the number given to her by Saleem hoping her father would answer. An older man answers and puts Anika's father on the phone. A dark skinned, tall slinky man sits on the torn mattress. Anika has a hard time understanding him because he talks really fast and his sentences make no sense. She questioned why he wasn't there for her as a child. All the blame went towards her mother.

"Your mother didn't want me there. She didn't want you to find out she was sleeping with Saleem. That's why she kicked me out and divorced me. I want Saleem dead. It's all your mother's fault," Masjid said.

"My mom never cheated on you! It was all in your head!" Anika said.

"Don't tell me what I can and can't do. I'm your father! I know everything! I know more than God! God looks up to me! You need to hear the truth. Your mother and Saleem should be dead! I want them to die! I loved you children and she didn't want me there. I was a good father. The only thing I did wrong was drink alcohol. Don't call me anymore! You're just as disrespectful as your mother!" Masjid said. Anika knows now that her father has a mental disorder. She drives over to Mosi's lavish apartment and he tries to comfort her.

"Are you going to take your medication now?" Mosi asked. Humiliation forced her to look away.

"I have no choice. I'm a lunatic," Anika said.

"No you're not Anika. There's nothing wrong with having a mental disorder. You're not crazy because you have to take medication," Mosi said.

"There's a big stigma of mental illness. People will look down on me," Anika said. Mosi takes her into his arms and held her as she begins to think about her financial situation.

"Mosi, I need help paying my credit card bills. They shortened my hours at work and I don't want to get bad credit," Anika said.

"No, I won't be able to help you," Mosi said as he hides two-hundred dollars in his underwear drawer. Ms. Sultan is peaking around the corner. She steps in to face Anika and Mosi.

"So what are you going to do Mosi?" Ms. Sultan asked.

"What am I going to do about what?" Mosi replied.

"You heard what she said. Her father's a lunatic and so is she," Ms. Sultan said. The shock hit Anika full force.

"I'm not leaving her if that's what you're implying," Mosi said.

"Aren't you going to stick up for me?!" Anika's words left her without restraint.

"Mom, I don't think you should be talking to her that way. She's not crazy. She's my future wife and I love her," Mosi said.

"You're going to regret this," Ms. Sultan said. Ms. Sultan leaves Mosi and begins to pack.

"Come on Keshia. Let's get the hell out of here!" Ms. Sultan said as she drags Keshia by the arm.

CHAPTER 9

Mary is home alone at 4am wondering where her boyfriend Mike could be. Mike comes home at 4:30am and heads straight for the shower. "Let me smell you," Mary said.
Mike backs away.

"What are you doing?" Mike questions.

"Where have you been?! I'm sick of this shit! You're always coming home late! Smelling like perfume! Mary screams.

"I'm not doing shit to you. You're paranoid," Mike said.

"What's her damn name?!" Mary grabs the phone and locks herself up in the bathroom. She dials Mike's voicemail. She hears a woman's voice.

"Hi Mike, it's Sharon. I wanted to make sure you got home safe. You were drunk from the alcohol." Mary redials the number.

"How do you know Mike?" Mary asked.

"We're just friends," Sharon said.

"Don't you know we live together? He has his clothes here," Mary said.

"I told you we just friends; stop calling here!" Sharon yells. Mary dials Sharon's number eight times and Sharon doesn't pick up the phone. Mary barges out of the bathroom door and begins to push Mike in the chest.

"What the hell are you doing? Who in the hell is she? You were supposed to be here with me!"

"She's a girl from my high school," Mike said.

"Why were you over her house at 4 o'clock in the morning?" Mike punches her in the nose and starts beating her in the face. Mary struggles to get away and runs into the kitchen and grabs a knife. Mike takes the knife from her, stabs her five times and then runs out the door. Mary phones Anika.

"Come over here! Mike just stabbed me!" Mary said. Anika hangs up the phone and calls the police. Anika and Mosi rushes over there and sees the ambulance and two police cars in Mary's driveway. One of the policemen walks up to Anika. "

"Can you tell me what happened here?" Anika pushes the policeman out of the way and heads for the ambulance. She sees Mary's body lying in the ambulance with a sheet covering her head.

"Oh my God! Oh my God! He killed her!" Anika screams. The policeman walks over to Anika.

"Tell us who killed her," the policeman demanded. Anika pushes him out the way again. Mary's mother and Rachel pull up in a Beetle and they immediately comfort her.

"How come you didn't tell me he was beating her?! I would have ended their relationship," Mary's mother said.

"I thought you knew," Anika said. Mosi jumps in Mary's mothers face.

"Don't go blaming her! She didn't kill her. Her boyfriend did," Mosi said. The policeman walks up to Anika again to question her. Anika turns her back on him.

"Anika you have to talk to him. Don't you want the man that did this to get arrested?" Mosi asked.

"Yes, I do," Anika said.

"Who did this? What can you tell me?" The police officer said.

"I thought me and Mary were dating the same person until I meet him recently. His name is Mike. He's been with Mary for two years now and has been abusing her. I told her to leave him. I told her he would do this," Anika said."Do you know where he lives?" the officer asked. Rachel steps closer.

"I do. He lives on Washington and 24th. Follow me, I can lead you to him," Rachel said.

"No, write down the address and we will find him," the police officer said. Three police cars immediately drive over to Mike's apartment. Mike sees them coming and starts shooting. The police return fire, hitting Mike in the arm. They then barge in and arrest him. Mike's mother witnesses the whole thing. She screams for the police to release him. She runs after the police car as they pull off, hitting the car window. A few days go by and Anika has to pull herself together to attend the funeral. She lies in Mosi's arms.

"I can't believe this happened. I don't know if I'm strong enough to go to this funeral," Anika said.

"You have to pull yourself together. I'm here for you Anika. I'm always here for you. I'm a good man," Mosi said. Anika and Mosi walk into the funeral and see Mary's mother and three sisters all sitting together in the first row. Mary's mom is wailing. Mike walks up to Anika. His mother bailed him out of jail.

"The nerve of him showing up at the funeral when he is guilty of killing Mary," Anika thinks.

"I don't know what happened to your friend. I received a call from her sister and I rushed right over. I'm so sorry for your lost," Mike said. Anika's arms swing in extreme force. Mosi has to hold her back.

"You are a lying piece of shit! Get the hell out of here! You shouldn't be here!" Anika screams.

"It's ok baby. We know the truth," Mosi said.

"The truth is I didn't kill her," Mike said.

"The police are looking for you, asshole. They say they now have a witness. I hope they lock your ass up for good," Anika said. The preacher walks up to Anika and places his hand on her shoulder.

"Yelling at him won't bring her back," the preacher said. Anika then walks up to Mary's mother and sisters and takes them by the hand.

"I'm so sorry for your loss," Anika said as tears shy away from her face.

"Please everyone, let's all have a seat. I'm sorry that we're here on this sad occasion. Death sometimes comes quickly and without warning. Mary has been visiting my church for ten years now and I hope what I taught her takes her to heaven. She was a beautiful soul, always there to help friends in need. From my understanding she was stabbed several times in the chest. The police say they have a lead. We will all miss her dearly." The preacher bows his head.

"Her mother and I were just talking about how she's grown into a beautiful woman. It's sad that someone took her away from us. She had just started teaching bible studies to the youth. They talked about how well she knew the bible and how much she helped them. I hope she is now with Jesus up in the sky. She left behind her mother and three sisters who we all care for very much. Mary was a good member of society. She always worked and paid her taxes on time. I remember when we went on vacation to Hawaii. I had choked on some food and she performed the Heimlich maneuver and saved my life. I could always count on Mary and so could members of this community. She started an organization called upward movement, which paid rent for the elderly. She raised one million dollars last year and had the support of many celebrities. We should all be thankful we had her in our lives."

The police then entered, proceeded toward Mike and arrested him.

"You haven't seen the last of me," he scowled. Anika watches as they drag Mike to the police car. Mike was later sentenced to life in prison for voluntary manslaughter.

CHAP T E R 1 0

Mosi and Tony pull up to the club. They step out of Mosi's Mercedes. Tony observes all the beautiful women in the club.

"So how do you feel about Mary's death? You two used to date," Mosi asked.

"I feel bad. Maybe if I would have stayed with her this wouldn't have happened," Tony said.

"It's not your fault. We always blame ourselves when someone dies. That's a natural reaction to death," Mosi said.

"So what's going on with Anika? Has she decided to take the medication?"

"I'm still trying to convince her that she's sick. Do you have any ideas?" Mosi asked.

"Take a picture or videotape her with your phone or camera if she has another relapse. After she gets hospitalized and treated show her the picture. And start giving her vitamins so she will be used to taking pills," Tony said.

"What?" Mosi questioned.

"My brother had a relapse and I took a picture of him. He saw that he was sick. You have to show people they're sick. Telling them won't work. Sometimes they don't remember all that they did." Tony said.

"I don't think she would forgive me if I did that," Mosi said.

"She would have to forgive you," Tony said. A young woman comes up to Mosi and hugs him. She wants to dance, but Mosi pushes her off. Tony sees this and grabs the girl by her arm and begins to dance. Mosi and Tony stay at the club until 5am. Anika is at Mosi's apartment huffing and puffing, waiting for Mosi to come home. In her mind, he has to be cheating.

"Why would a man stay at a club this late to just drink and dance?" Anika thinks. Anika remembers Andrew and gives him a call.

"Hey, this is Anika."

"Oh, I thought you wouldn't call me. And it's late! Something is wrong, what is it?" Andrew asked.

"My fiancé is still out to some club. Do you think all men cheat?" Anika carefully listens to his answer. She learned through her Psychology class that if a man says all men cheat then it's because he cheats and he cannot be trusted. She knows that unless he has done some type of research, there's no way he can be sure of the answer.

"Hell yeah, all men cheat! What do you think he's doing right now? No man would stay out all night unless he's getting some booty. Believe me when I used to go to the clubs I would pick up a girl each night. I'd do what I had to do with her and then I would go back to the same club and pick up another woman. Believe me, he's cheating," Andrew said.

"Do you have anyone now?" Anika questioned. "I got you right? Let me take you out. Let me spend money on you. Let me get your nails and toes done," Andrew said.

This sounds too good to Anika. Mosi never takes her to get her toes and nails done. She wants a man to take care of her.

"No you don't have any morals. I'm not dating you," Anika said.

"What do you mean?" Andrew asked out of curiosity.

"You asked me to sleep with you for two-hundred dollars. I wouldn't do that," Anika said.

"Well, don't you think two-hundred dollars is too much to ask for in the beginning of a relationship?" Andrew asked.

"I didn't ask you for money," Anika hears keys and hangs up on Andrew. Mosi and Tony walk in intoxicated. Tony is holding Mosi up. Anika can smell the stench from Mosi's breath.

"Why in the hell are you out at some club this late when you know I'm here waiting for you?!"

"I can do whatever the hell I want to do! Me and Tony are going on a vacation," Mosi said.

"What? Can I go?" Anika said.

"Yeah, you can go," Mosi said. Tony steps closer to Anika.

"Why does she have to go? Don't bring her?" Tony said.

"Yeah, Anika. You can stay here," Mosi said.

"You know what? I've had enough of your shit. It's over. I don't want to be with your ass anymore." Anika begins to hear her voices again.

"You see Anika, Mosi doesn't want you. He's cheating on you. Nobody wants you. You're a loser. You need to finish yourself off. Do us all a favor and kill yourself. Your mother thinks you're nuts. Mosi thinks you're nuts. Tony thinks you're nuts. What does that add up to? You're nuts. End it!" Other voices join in. *"End it! End it! End it!"* Anika holds her hands against the side of her head.

"What's wrong Anika?" Mosi asked.

"I'm going to kill myself," Anika said.

Anika storms out of the apartment and heads for her mother's house. She has absolutely no intentions on killing herself. She wants to punish Mosi for cheating eventhough she has no proof. Mosi heads straight for a can of beer.

"What are you doing man? You're already drunk. If you drink anymore, you just may kill yourself." Tony said.

"I know what I'm doing. I love that woman. I want her as my wife," Mosi said.

"Well, if you keep drinking you won't have her as your wife. You'll be dead." Mosi pushes Tony to the side and heads for his car. The car is swerving as Mosi drives over to Anika's house. Anika lets him in and he runs to the toilet and vomits. He tries to sleep in the same bed as Anika but she pushes him out of the bed and he falls onto the floor.

"I don't want you no more! The wedding is off! You never could set a date anyway. You never wanted to get married!" Anika said.

"Sometimes I want to marry you, sometimes I don't. You're a hard person to get along with Anika. I love you so much. I'm hurting bad. I need you," Mosi said.

"You don't need me!" Anika screams and pushes him out of her room, then slams the door. He goes to sleep on the couch. In the morning Anika's mother is shocked to see him.

"Mosi, what are you doing here?" Ms. Muhammad asked.

"Anika said she doesn't want me anymore. She said she's going to kill herself," Mosi said.

"If it was anyone else I would say take that suicide attempt seriously, but with Anika, she used to say that to me all the time and never meant it. You know how Anika loves drama? That's one reason she's so sick. Why do you think she used to hang around Mary all the time? Mary was a drama queen and so is Anika. So what did you do wrong?" Ms. Muhammad asked.

"I didn't come home until 5 in the morning," Mosi said.

"Now you know you're about to get married. Do you expect to be coming home late until 5am when you get married?" Ms. Muhammad asked.

"I never thought about that. I guess once I get married, I shouldn't be out in the clubs," Mosi said.

"Why wait until you get married? Are you sure you're ready for marriage? And don't think you're ready for a marriage if you're still clubbing. What's there to do at a club, but drink and pick up women? Isn't that why you men go to clubs?" Ms. Muhammad asked.

"I used to go for the woman, but now I go for the alcohol and the music," Mosi said.

"Are you an alcoholic?" Ms. Muhammad asked.

"That's a possibility," Mosi said.

"Maybe Anika will go to alcoholics anonymous with you?" Ms. Muhammad said.

"Yea, I'll ask her," Mosi said.

"I think you should go to work. Life is 1% what happens to you and 99% how you react to it. You have to learn how to channel that energy into something positive. Some people are called to change the world? The lifestyle you're leading is killing you. Anika and I have relatives who have died from liver disease due to alcohol addiction. Now, think about that while you're at work. I'll make things right with Anika," Ms. Muhammad said. Mosi leaves for work. Anika was listening to the entire conversation. She steps out into the living room.

"Are you taking his side Mama?" Anika questioned.

"You should have first asked why Mosi was late instead of assuming he was cheating. You should not base your life decisions on assumptions. You should always find out the truth first and then react to the truth. There will be a whole lot of less break ups, less fights, less broken promises if people did that. Are you faithful Anika?" Ms. Muhammad asked.

"I am talking to someone else but I'm not cheating," Anika said.

"If you're engaged there should be no reason to call this other man. You're already cheating," Ms. Muhammad said. Anika's scrunched up nose leads her to work. A very attractive man stops her before she makes it to her desk.

"I'm a TV producer. What would you say if I told you that I want you to do some acting for me? You're too beautiful to be working here," Hameed said. Anika smiles.

"How much does it pay?" Anika asked.

"You would work for free and you will learn how to become a TV producer. I want every one of my actors to become a producer," Hameed said.

"Oh, I don't know if I could be a TV producer," Anika said.

"Come into my office and read a script. I'll tell your boss you'll be a little late." Hameed hands Anika the script. He trips over the computer to see if he could distract her. This is a technique teachers use to see if actors can keep going without being distracted. He gave her the script and she began reading her lines.

"Do you think that a child can be smart enough to build a computer? Well, I do. There are a few things that you will need. Oh, this is easy I can do this," Anika said.

"We're taping our next show on Saturday July 23. Come to the show; here's the address and sign up for the producer's class." Later on that evening Anika lets herself into Mosi's apartment and takes all of her things. Mosi arrives later and sees that all of Anika things are gone. He then begins to rip up the pictures they had taken together.

Anika is excited about acting in her first television show. She buys a blue top from New York and Company and wears jeans to match. When she first walks into the studio, she is greeted by the makeup artist and is led into the studio's dressing room. There are many people there waiting to get their first taste of stardom. Hameed, the TV producer, walks in and signals for Anika to walk his way. She is given a tour of the studio. Where she will be acting, there are three highly expensive HD cameras. The one marked, 'number one,' has a teleprompter. Anika notices her script is up and ready.

"Have you ever acted before Anika?" Hameed asked.

"Yes, I have. I was selected to be in the PCCA program at Gibbs high school for the artistically talented. I'm a natural, but I never had the passion to pursue that career after high school. I think I would be a better TV producer than an actor. After high school, I'd shoot music videos with family and really enjoyed that," Anika said.

"Well, here is your chance to see which one you like better. I want you to stand behind that line and read off the teleprompter," Hameed said.
Anika was extremely nervous. She took a few breaths and began to read.

"Did you know that anyone could build a computer? You can go to an electronics store and buy the individual parts you need-" "Cut," Hameed said.

"You have slurred speech I need you to slow down and enunciate. And you left out the opening part," Hameed said. Anika took a few breaths and began again.

"Hello, I'm your co-host Anika and you're watching, Build Your Own PC. Did you know that anyone could build a computer?" "That was good Anika. I want you to follow me so you can sign up for your TV producing class." Anika followed Hameed to the front of the building and paid her thirty-five dollars to take her TV producing class to become a certified TV producer.

CHAPTER 11

A few months have gone by and Anika starts dating Andrew. Andrew invites Anika over to his house.

"I knew he was cheating on you," Andrew said.

"Well, I still haven't proved that. Do you think I'm crazy Andrew?" Anika questions.

"No, once when I was in jail I wanted to leave that place so I started praying to God to take me away. Don't you know he actually put me into the stars? I was in the stars baby," Andrew said.

"You weren't in the stars, you were seeing the stars with your third eye. So what did you go to jail for?" Anika questions.

"Oh, because of a few unpaid parking tickets. Nothing major," Andrew said.

"Baby come here and sit on my lap. Tell me about this producing class," Andrew said. Anika places herself on his lap. She wraps her arms around his neck.

"I have to go there tonight," Anika said.

"You know I'll do anything for you," Andrew said. He starts to kiss her on her neck.

"Look, I can't be in a committed relationship with you. We can have sex, but I can't be committed to you," Anika said.

"Why is that Anika?" Andrew questioned.

"Because I don't think you would be faithful to me. I think you would cheat," Anika said.

"Ok, we can have that understanding. I have to be honest with you. When I first met you I was trying to use you. I just wanted you for sex but I changed my mind. I fell in love with you." Andrew undresses Anika. Anika then takes off Andrews's pants and underwear. His Johns was no bigger than her index finger. She thought about backing out.

"Why have sex? I don't feel anything anyway, since I was molested as a child. But I'm curious. Mosi is the only man I've ever had sex with. I want to know what it's like to have sex with another man," Anika thought. Andrew enters her and it's all over in one minute. This is the second man that she has ever had sex with. She could have done without it, but she got her revenge on Mosi. She can't wait to tell Mosi what she had done. She wants him to feel the pain she felt when he stayed out all night. The next morning Anika meets up with Rachel.

"So now you realize that Mosi just might be a good man?" Rachel said.

"Yes, but now I'm dating someone else and we just had sex," Anika said.

"Oh my God! Wasn't Mosi the only one you ever slept with?" Rachel asked.

"Yes. I was always curious what it would be like to sleep with another man. Now I wish I would not have done that," Anika said.

"How much do you know about this guy you're sleeping with?" Rachel said.

"I've known him for three months," Anika said.

"Look him up," Rachel said.

"What?" Anika questioned.

"Look him up. What's his name?" Rachel asked.

"Andrew Black," Anika said. Rachel pulls out her laptop and opens up the Internet. She lands on a page where you can do an inmate search.

"What are you doing?" Anika asked.

"I'm looking him up. I'm seeing if he has a record, Andrew Black right?" Rachel said.

"Yes." Rachel pulls up an arrest record for Andrew. He was arrested for residential burglary and assault.

"Do you see what I'm seeing?" Rachel asked.

"Yes, that's him alright. He told me he had a few parking tickets that he didn't pay and that's why he got arrested," Anika said in shock.

"What are you going to do?" Rachel asked.

"Leave him the hell alone," Anika said.

A week went by and Anika would just ignore Andrew's phone calls. She checked her mail and there was a letter in it from Mosi. She begins to read. "Baby I know you think I'm unfaithful, but I'm not. I want you back. We have something special. Remember the first day we met? It was in our business class. You were afraid to talk to me. You were so beautiful; like a blossoming flower. Look how far you've come. Please don't be upset because I'm going to the clubs. I'm not looking for another woman. You're all the woman I need. Come back to me baby. I'll treat you right. Do you think another man could do the things that I can do for you? I gave you your first brand new car. That was a good car.

Instead of keeping it for myself, I gave it to you and I got another car for myself. Remember when you crossed the bridge for the first time in your car? God must have been on your side because you were not even looking before you switched lanes. You think that I think you are crazy, but I've never called you that. Stop listening to your friends and believing what they say. I'm here for you. You're the only one that I want. I'm going to go to Las Vegas for a little while. I want you to come back into my life. Call me when you get this letter. I want us to get back together."

Anika drops the letter and heads over to Mosi's apartment. Mosi is excited to see her. They began hugging and kissing and they made love. Anika looks into Mosi's eyes.

"I had sex with someone else." Mosi's heart was crushed for a second.

"Was he better than me?" Mosi asked.

"No, he wasn't. It was a very bad experience Mosi; I should never have done it." Anika replied. The phone began to ring. Anika picks it up and it's Andrew on the other end. She forgot that she had used Mosi's phone to call him one night.

"Don't call here anymore," Anika said.

"But we made love," Andrew said.

"Who is that?" Mosi asked. "It's the guy I slept with," Anika said. The phone rings again.

"Stop calling," Anika said.

"Why are you doing this to me?!" Andrew screamed. Andrew had been following her so he knew she was at Mosi's apartment. Anika leaves for her producer's class. Andrew follows her. She steps out of her car and heads for her class when he walks over and takes her by the arm.

"Why are you doing this to me? I fell in love with you," Andrew said.

"Remember we were not in a committed relationship. I can see whom ever I want. Why are you following me? You said yourself that you were trying to use me for sex anyway. It's not my fault that you got hurt," Anika said.

"So you don't love me?" Andrew asked.

"No Andrew, I don't," Anika said.

"Then I'll leave you alone," Andrew said. He gets into his car and drives off. She never sees him again. Anika enters her producer's class.

"There are different shots that you can take with your camera. A close up shot is shooting at someone's waist. A long shot is shooting from head to toe. An extreme close up is shooting someone's face. Then you have a knee shot which is self-explanatory. My favorite shot is the over the shoulder shot. This looks the most professional. You'll see this in movies.

"Anika stand right here," Mr. Brown said. Anika stands in front of the camera.

"Ok, I'm going to run back and forth. I want you to capture my movement," Mr. Brown said. Mr. Brown looks at the monitor to see if Anika is keeping up. Anika is having a hard time keeping up with him.

"See Anika you have to look at the person's waist so that you can tell which way they're going. And you have to stand at just the right distance from the person to be able to capture the whole body. This is what we're going to do. I want each of you to work at the different stations, audio, technical board, show host, camera, lighting, editing, and see which one you love the best."

When Anika was young, she had this drive to buy a camera. And when she finally bought one she started directing home movies. She never knew that she would end up a certified TV producer. She works every station and falls in love with hosting. She thinks to herself.

"What type of TV show can I produce? I'm a writer. I want to live out my dream. Maybe I should call it, "Living my Dreams." Yeah, I think that's what I will do. I can email the famous people I like and see if one of them will allow me to film them. I know. I'll email Mikel Soul/ Hop. I don't know him, but if he allows me to interview him then I know I can be a TV producer because he is famous. He's number one in Germany."

Anika hastens over to her house to email Mikel Soul/Hop. "Mikel I am a huge fan of yours. I'm a TV producer. My show will air in two hundred thousand households every week. I'd like to discuss the possibility of interviewing you. I would be much appreciative. My number is 555-4324." One week after that email Mikel emails her agreeing to do the interview. Mosi went to Las Vegas and didn't even tell her if he made it safe. This really infuriates Anika, but she has to keep her mind together in order to do an effective interview. Jswift has opened up for Mikel Soul/Hop. Jswift is an African American, with slender built, and in his early twenties. He sings his song, "Heatin' it up," then Mikel takes the stage. The girls began to scream and pull their chairs up to the stage. Mikel is a slender Italian in his late twenty's. Anika and the camera man, Robert, go outside to set up the camera. Robert sets up the tripod. Anika sets up the microphone.

"Testing, testing," Anika said.

"I think we're ready," Robert said. Jswift walks outside.

"You're going to be the next to make it Jswift," Anika said.

"I think so too," Jswift said.

"Are you ready? I'm going to ask you a few questions," Anika said.

"Yes, I'm ready," Jswift said.

"Heatin' it up," is that yours? You wrote that?" Anika asked.

"Yes, that's my new song. We're going hard with it. It's playing in all the clubs, DJ's, radio, blog sites. We are going all in on it," Jswift said.

"Ah man that song is hot. So have you had a chance to upload it on 95.7 yet?" Anika said.

"No, not yet. I know a few people there so I'll bring them a copy. Hopefully they can respect it and see the hustle and potential in the project and help me push it to the right people. I'll let the Tampa Bay area decide on the track. I feel like this can be the one," Jswift said.

"Ok, I think so, I think this is it. I've heard your song before, but it didn't hit me like it did tonight and I guess it's because I saw you perform it. The song is hot. It really is. Oh yeah, you're gonna make it, for sure. It might take up to a few years for the song to become known, but it'll happen. So where are you from?" Anika asked.

"I'm from South Tampa," Jswift said.

"So you were born and raised in Tampa?"

"I was born in Orlando and moved to Tampa. I have been here since I was two," Jswift said.

"So did you ever get vocal lessons?" Anika asked.

"No, I was self-taught," Jswift said.

"You're a genius," Anika said.

"Everybody has their own talents you just have to find them and explore them," Jswift said.

"Whenever you don't take voice lessons and you're that good, that lets you know you got something special," Anika said. Mikel walks past the audience. Several of the young girls pull on his shirt. His bodyguards protect him as he walks outside towards Anika."I can't believe I have the opportunity to interview you. This is like a dream come true for me," Anika said.

"It's my pleasure," Mikel said.

"What's up, this is Anika and you're watchin' Livin' my Dreams. I got international artist, Mikel Soul/Hop in the building. How are you doing?" Anika asked.

"I'm doing great. How are you?" Mikel asked.

"I'm good. I see you are all blinged out. Who are you wearing?" Anika asked.

"I got a lot of sponsors that provide clothing for me," Mikel said.

"I love your belt," Anika said. "It's specially made. I'll probably get my name engraved on it pretty soon. A jeweler made this for me so it's one of a kind," Mikel said.

"So where are you from?" Anika asked.

"I'm originally from Kansas City, Missouri," Mikel said.

"Why did you move down here?" Anika asked.

"My record label found me. They believed I was the next artist to make it big," Mikel said.

"So how long have you been with your label?" Anika asked.

"I've lived here for about eight months now. They really believe in me and they're doing a good job of supporting me," Mikel said.

"How long you have been singing?" Anika asked. "Since I was about eight years old. I started singing in church. They told me I had a beautiful voice and wanted me to sing every Sunday. It was a southern black church," Mikel said.

"And you're rapping now, too," Anika said.

"Yeah, I rap a little bit. I do both. That's why it's Mikel Soul/Hop. I do soul and hip hop," Mikel said.

"So let's talk about your CD. When was it produced?"

"The CD just came out. It's all over the Tampa Bay area and I have a hit that's been on several local stations in addition to being played internationally. I have my own DJ and promoter that are really pushing it right now. I did all the graphics too, if you notice it's not too bad," Mikel said.

"That's awesome! Ok, it's time to wrap it up. Thank you so much for allowing me to interview you. This has been a dream come true for me," Anika said. "Thank you," Mikel said and gives her a hug.

Mosi finally calls Anika.

"Why didn't you call me so I knew you arrived safely? And why did you wait two days to call me?"

"What are you doing in Las Vegas? What's so important that you can't call me?"

"You should know better than that. It's like you're a child. I have to baby you for you to do the right things. You better not have a woman in your room. I'm the reason this relationship is still lasting. If it weren't for me we wouldn't even be together. I carry us. I don't do anything wrong. You're always missing in action," Anika said. Mosi says nothing.

"I'll talk to you later," Anika said. Anika hangs up the phone. Mosi is in the room with Tony.

"I'm done with her. She's so controlling. She talks to me like I'm a child and she always thinks I'm cheating on her. I've had enough of her. It's over," Mosi said.

"Well, ain't you gonna tell the bitch?" Tony said.

"I was told by my mom you never hurt a girl but maybe I should tell her it's over," Mosi said.

CHAP T E R 1 2

Anika gets on her favorite social media site to find more talent. She got lucky with Mikel so maybe she will get some more luck. After searching for hours her tired fingers stop on a young man's page. His name is Solo and he's a solo rapper. His music is quite unique. It's much different than what she is used to. She emails him and he emails her right back.

"We have a video shoot scheduled with a very famous artist. I want you to fly to Miami to catch the video and get an interview," Solo said. Anika immediately phoned her employer to ask for a few days off. They granted her a week's vacation so she catches a plane with her assistant, Robert, to Miami.

"Set up the camera. I want to do a quick opening. What's up you're watching living my dreams. I'm definitely living my dreams. I'm all the way in Miami getting ready to interview a very, very famous artist. As you know I brought you Mikel and Jswift and music by Rino all the way from Europe, so you know I got some hot artist for you. So sit back, relax, and we about to get poppin'. Does that sound good Robert? Or should we do another take?" Anika said.

"No, not at all, that sounds good," Robert said. Robert puts away the camera and they both head over the bridge to meet up with Solo. They both greet each other with a hug and Anika follows Solo to the video shoot.

"Soulja P, this is Anika," Solo said. Anika is speechless. She cannot believe that she has the opportunity to meet Soulja P. This is another dream come true. Hands trembles as she gets out her microphone.

"Is it ok to interview you?" Anika questioned.

"Sure, it's ok Mama," Soulja P said.

"What's up this Anika and you're watchin', 'Living my Dreams.' I got Soulja P in the building. How're you doing?" Anika asked.

"Hey, what's going on this your boy Soulja P based out of Wick city, Florida you know we doing big out here," Soulja P said.

"So where did you get your name? What does it mean?" Anika asked.

"Soulja P stands for Soulja Philosophy. It basically comes from coming from the streets going through a lot of stuff and having the Philosophy of a Soulja, getting through it all. When times get tough you gotta keep going," Soulja P said.

"So you grew up in a bad neighborhood?" Anika asked..

"Yes, I grew up in a really bad neighborhood. I went through a lot of things when I was young. And it developed me into the person I am today. I try to use it to my advantage by bringing my experiences into my lyrics and creating music that can help people who are going through the same things I went through," Soulja P said.

"I was reading your biography and it said you used to be in the streets a lot. What kind of advice can you give to these young kids in the streets selling drugs and doing the wrong things?" Anika asked.

"The best thing I can tell them is to stay in sports, stay involved and go to school. Because if you're not in school, you're not involved and the only thing you can do is get in trouble. You gotta have some kind of passion, some kind of dream, something to work towards, otherwise you're just going to go down the wrong path. Going down the rocky road is pretty much what I call it," Soulja P said.

"So what songs are you performing tonight at the Fluid Lounge?" Anika asked.

"Tonight I'm going to do up and around. I got a new song called so thick and I'm going to do pop," Soulja P said.

"Ok, I'm looking forward to it," Anika said.

"Yep, we're gonna get it on tonight," Soulja P said.

"Thank you for coming on the show with me," Anika said.

"Thank you for coming out and for the interview. I'm definitely happy to see y'all out here." Soulja P said.

"Alright," Anika said.

"Thank you so much for the interview. When will it air?" Soulja P asked.

"It will air for an entire month, once a week on Saturday at 11pm worldwide. We reach 200,000 households," Anika said. Anika's ratings were high. Everybody was watching her show, but the only way her show would get picked up is if she had financing to buy a HD camera and money to travel to more locations. She already had a major artist on her show and the show is local. That was a major accomplishment. Anika's mother picks her up from the airport.

"So how did it go?" Ms. Muhammad asked.

"I can't believe it mama. I got a major artist on my show and I'm a nobody," Anika said.

"Don't say that. A lot of people know you already. To me, you already made it," Ms. Muhammad said.

"I would make it if I had financing," Anika said. "Go to the rehabilitation center. They help disabled people finance new businesses, but make sure you do a business plan first. They will turn you down if you don't have a good business plan. Go to the University of South Florida business program and have them help you with a business plan," Ms. Muhammad said. Anika feels like this is her destiny; that this center is going to take her all the way to the top. She made an appointment for the re-habilitation center, but doesn't take her mother's advice to do a business plan. She comes empty handed. She sees her counselor walking towards her, an African American woman in her forties. She dresses in corporate wear, a button down shirt, and pressed slacks. Felisha looks down at Anika's shoes. Anika is dressed in casual wear and has on slippers. She was too lazy to dress up for her interview. She didn't realize how important first impressions are.

"Hello Anika. What is it you would like to do?" Felisha asked.

"I want funding to pay for equipment so I can start a film production company. I plan to film music videos and interview famous artists. With the equipment I can tape my show in HD and present it to the networks," Anika said.

"You should do it for free. You'll never make it as a TV producer," Felisha said. Anika's soul was crushed by someone who has never even seen her in action. Anika shed tears of pain.

"Here go to the university and meet with a business coach to develop a business plan," Felisha said.

Anika set up a meeting with a business coach. He looked over her business plan and told her it would never work. She was lost. Her dreams were crushed. This made her lose her passion and her drive. Anika sits in her room, staring at the floor. Upon entering the room, her mother enters the room and sees how upset she is.

"What happened Anika? Why are you crying?" Ms. Muhammad said.

"The rehabilitation center won't give me financing for my TV show. She told me to do it for free. She said it would never work and that I will never make it as a TV producer. I give up, Mama. I've lost my drive," Anika said.

"Did you present a good business plan?" Ms. Muhammad asked.

"No, I did not," Anika said.

"The only reason you haven't made it yet is because you don't listen. You do what you want to instead of listening to professional advice. You do as you wish and not what is required to do. Maybe you should save up your money and do it on your own," Ms. Muhammad said.

"I'm afraid I will never be that good. The passion is gone. I just don't want to do it anymore," Anika said.

"Success doesn't happen overnight. It could take you thirty years to make it. Don't allow a dream killer to stop you. You have a gift Anika. Not everyone can produce their own TV show.

You've interviewed Mikel, Jswift, and Soulja P. That's huge. Please don't quit," Ms. Muhammad said.

"I will try, but it's going to be hard to get my passion back," Anika said.

CHAP TE R 1 3

Anika dreams of a car driving fast. It's Mosi in the car with
friends. A blue car passes Mosi's car and all Anika could think is
for Mosi to slow down. Anika is used to her dreams coming true,
so she tries to call and tell Mosi not to drink and drive like he
always does, but Mosi doesn't answer the phone. Anika knows
he's back in town because Rachel told her she saw him. She
drives over to Mosi's apartment and Mosi answers the door.

"I really missed you Mosi. Why you didn't tell me you
were in town?" Anika questioned.

"I just got back," Mosi said. Anika's female instincts told
her something was strange. Something just was not right, but
she missed him and wanted to make love and so they did. After-
wards, she went to watch television and realized the picture of
her and Mosi was lying flat on top of the television set.
She thought that was weird, but she didn't say anything. She
went to the garbage can to throw away her food and the garbage can smelled really bad like something died in there. She
had the key to Mosi's apartment so she thought she can come
back to his apartment while he's at work and see what stunk so
bad. Mosi went off to work and that's exactly what she did.
She used her key to let herself in and went straight to the
garbage can. She picked out a few rotten apples and set them
aside. There was a paper towel hiding something. She unravels
the paper towel and finds a condom with russet stains at the
tip. She finally got her proof that Mosi had been cheating on
her. There's no way he could deny it this time, she had proof.
She knew he was no good. Now she has evidence. Her voices
start to weigh in on her.

98

"We told you he was no good. Now you know. What are you going to do now? You're a loser. You don't have anyone now. Why don't you do us all a favor and end it all. Mosi would be happy. You see he has another girl. He was always cheating on you. Now you have proof, proof of his infidelity. Now what are you going to do? No one wants you. You're a loser. Just finish yourself off." Voices join in. *"Do it, do it, do it."* Anika receives a call from Rachel.

"Mosi's cheating on me Rachel. I found a condom in his garbage can," Anika said.

"Oh my God! What are you going to do?" Rachel asked.

"I'm going to leave him, that's what I'm going to do. It's over. Now I have proof and he can't deny it. I'm going to wait here until he comes home," Anika said. Anika waits for eight hours before he finally makes it home.

"I found this in your garbage can," Anika hands him the condom. Mosi's heart sank.

"You went through my things?" Mosi asked.

"Yes, I did. Explain this. You cheated on me?" Anika said.

"I'm gay," Mosi said. What he was saying was too traumatic for her to comprehend. It just went in one ear and out the other one.

"What's her name? How could you do this to me? Where did you meet her?"

Mosi lies. "At the bar," Mosi said.

"How could you do this to me?" Anika said.

"Before we were serious, years ago, I would sleep with another woman. And after we got serious I had oral sex with someone, but I never cheated on you back then," Mosi said.

99

"If you had oral sex then you cheated on me. I can't believe you," Anika begins to cry and Mosi goes down on her. They both lay together in the same bed he betrayed her in.

CHAP T E R 1 4

Mosi meets Tony at a club. "Anika found out I cheated on her," Mosi said. "So did she break up with you?" Tony asked. "No, she didn't," Mosi said. "Well are you two getting married?" Tony said.

"Sometimes I want to marry her and sometimes I don't. I don't know what to do," Mosi drinks a long island ice tea.

"Don't drink that man. It'll have you drunk and you know I'm already drunk so you have to drive," Tony said.

"I can drink and drive. I do it all the time," Mosi said.

"Alright, let's go to your place and smoke some marijuana," Tony said.

"Alright," Mosi said. Mosi and Tony get into the Mercedes Benz and Mosi begins speeding.

"Let's see how fast this baby can go," Mosi said. They both begin laughing. Mosi pushes the pedal to 90 miles per hour.

"Go faster Mosi. There's no one on the road," Tony said. He pushes it to 100 then 110 then 140. A blue car passes by and then cuts them off. Mosi breaks to slow down. Mosi's car hydroplanes across the grass and off the road. The car runs into the light pole. Their heads hit the dashboard in slow motion.

"Ah man you alright?" Mosi asked.
"Yes, You?" Tony asked.

"Yes, I'm alright," Mosi said. Mosi gets out the car to see the damage. The hood of the car is dented in.

"We gotta call a tow truck man. You go home first," Mosi said. The tow truck came in 45 minutes and picked up Mosi and Tony. Mosi gets home and see's Anika on the couch. His head is bleeding and Anika runs up to him.

"Oh my God, what happened?" Anika asked.

"A blue car cut us off and I lost control of the car," Mosi said.

"I was gonna tell you about my dream, but I got distracted. I was supposed to tell you to slow down Mosi."

Mosi goes into his underwear drawer and pulls out a large bag of marijuana. He rolls up a joint and lights it up.

"What are you doing Mosi?" Anika asked.

"I'm smoking," Mosi said.

"Well, I can see that. But what are you smoking?" Anika questioned.

"This is marijuana," Mosi said.

"Mosi, I can't believe you're smoking," Anika said.

"You want some?" Anika thought about it.

"No, I promised my mom, I wouldn't do drugs," Anika said.

"I'm hungry, I'm going to go get some donuts," Anika said.

"At two o'clock in the morning? I'm sorry Anika I got you high," Mosi said.

"Damn Mosi I'll be right back." Mosi begins to laugh. Anika looks at the damage done to the car. She drives over to the donut shop. Two policemen sit in their cars. Anika hopes they don't smell her.

"Let me have two crispy creams," Anika said. The cashier is a gay white male in his twenty's.

"You're Mosi's girl, aren't you?" the cashier said.

"Yes," Anika said.

"Mm hmm," the cashier said. Anika leaves for her car.

When Anika enters the apartment it is filled with smoke. She struggles to open a window. The window is jammed and won't open. Mosi is sitting on the couch watching a movie, laughing hard.

"What's so funny Mosi?" Anika asked.

"You should try watching this movie when you're high. Everything is so clear. You notice things that you didn't notice before. See directors use subliminal messages in their movies. They give you little signs," Mosi said.

"You're just high Mosi," Anika said.

Mosi runs into the bedroom and takes off all his clothes and comes running into the living room but naked. He runs as he laughs.

"I was a spider man Anika! You should have seen me! I was flying!" Mosi said.

"Mosi you're high and you're drunk. Come to bed," Anika said. Anika and Mosi lie down to go to sleep. She tosses and turns, but just cannot sleep. She thinks her fiancé has camera's up. She thinks she is being watched. She lies on her back and looks up and in her third eye, she sees a brown teddy bear floating. She thinks God is trying to calm her down. She pushes Mosi with great strength. "It's time," Anika said. Anika takes off her bra and underwear and sit in the windowsill nude. She points at the cars that are driving by. No one looks up. No one sees her. She doesn't have on her contacts so everything is a blur. She focuses on the purple she sees through the window. She picks up the bible and opens it to the pages of Noah and lays the bible in the dresser drawer. She takes a cup of water and places it on the light bulb in the hallway.

Beth, her spirit guide begins to speak to her, "Anika everyone will know you. Celebrities will come for you. You will be well known and a billionaire. You must hide your resume. People can't know how you made it," Beth said.

Anika takes her resume and a lighter and walks into the bathroom.

She sets the resume on fire. The fire alarm goes off.

"Anika what are you doing?!" Mosi screams and puts out the fire.

"Rashid! Rashid!" Anika screams her brother's name. In her mind, she's quiet.

"Anika I think you're high from the marijuana," Mosi said. Mosi is scared and grabs the bag of marijuana and flushes it down the toilet.

"Rashid! Rashid!" Anika begins to cry. Anika massages her hair. Mosi takes a picture of her using his Polaroid.

"Anika you're sick again," Mosi said.

"No, I'm not." Anika keeps screaming. She doesn't realize how sick, she is. She doesn't realize she was sitting in the window seal naked and she blocks out calling her brother's name. She sees Mosi heading towards her with a pillow. She doesn't know what he does next because she blocks it out.

"I have to go to work," Anika said.

She wears what she wore the first day as an actress, her blue shirt and jeans. Employees are only allowed to wear jeans on Friday and today is Monday but Anika has lost her mind... again. She gets into her car and heads to work. She gets on the highway. She thinks she is leading all the cars. She thinks everyone is following her. When she makes it to work she parks in the CEO's parking spot.

She thinks she owns the company. She gets the attention of one of the employees. She whispers.

"Everyone should be listening to 95.7 the beat. I work there," the employee gives her a look of confusion and then walks away. She attempts to pass by the security guards.

"You can't park there. You're going to have to move your car," the security guard says. Anika begins to cry and walks towards her desk. She sits there crying. Her supervisor sees her and helps her out of the seat. He walks her back towards the security guards.

"I have to pee," Anika said.

"I'll wait for you," the supervisor said. Anika uses the restroom and then walks up to her supervisor. He walks her to the security guards.

"What's wrong?" the security guard asked. Anika doesn't say a word; she just looks at him.

"Is it safe for you to drive?" the security guard asked.

"Yes," Anika said. She drives back over to Mosi's apartment.

"You scared me! You need to take your medication. Look at you," Mosi said. Mosi hands her a picture of herself. For the first time Anika sees what's in those textbooks. She sees a person, not crazy, but a person with a mental disorder.

"Take your medication, please," Mosi said. Anika takes the medication, cries, and hugs Mosi.

"I'm sick baby. I need help," Anika said. Mosi takes her by the hand and walks her to the car. He opens the car door for her.

"I'm going to get you some help," Mosi said. Mosi

takes her to a mental health center. They both stand in line. It's a long line. There are ten people ahead of them. Years ago, Anika would see people that have lost their minds walking the streets, talking to themselves, but not anymore because of this mental health facility. You don't see anyone wandering the streets anymore. After about thirty minutes, Anika and Mosi make it to the front of the line.

"We need help," Mosi said.

"Have you been here before?" the intake specialist asked.

"No," Anika responded.

"Follow me," the intake specialist said. She takes her to the nurse practitioner's office.

"Hello, I'm Diane. How can I help you?"

"I have paranoid schizophrenia and I need more medication," Anika said.

"Tell me about your childhood," Diane said.

"I was molested by my brother. Then he committed suicide," Anika said.

"What are you paranoid about?" Diane asked.

"I sometimes think my fiancé is cheating on me and last night I thought he had cameras up.

"Are you susceptible to stress?" Diane asked.

"Yes," Anika said.

"How is your sleep?" Diane asked.

"I sometimes get excited and can't sleep. I'll be up for two days and won't even feel tired," Anika said.

"Do you have mood swings?" Diane asked.

"No. My mood stays pretty much the same. I never got counseling for the molestation. I think I need therapy," Anika said.

"Do you feel guilty?" Diane said.

"No," Anika said. Diane is quiet.

"What's her diagnosis Diane?" Mosi asked.

"You don't have paranoid schizophrenia, you have schizoaffective bipolar type," Diane said.

"Does she need medication?" Mosi asked.

"Yes for the rest of her life. I'm prescribing 50 mg of Clomipramine and 160 mg of Geodon to be taken daily. Anika looks at Mosi and smiles.

"You're gonna be ok," Mosi said.

"Yes, I am," Anika said. Anika took the medication for a week and the voices went away. She makes another appointment with Diane.

"So how is the medication?" Diane asked. Anika begins to smile.

"The voices are gone. I feel normal again," Anika said.

"Do you work?" Diane asked.

"Yes full time," Anika said.

"I think you should quit your job and get on disability. The stress of the job may make you have another relapse even if you're taking your medication. What do you do for fun?" Diane asked.

"I'm a certified TV producer and I just started writing a book about my true life story," Anika said.

"What you are describing is positive stress. You can have hobbies and make money off your hobbies and not have to work. Working a job you don't like will bring you stress, but if you can find jobs that bring you positive stress and put your energy in them, you won't have a breakdown," Diane said.

"I have a good paying job and I don't want to lose it, but I'll give it some thought," Anika said.

The next day Anika prepares herself for work. She can't take her mind off what the nurse practitioner told her about getting on disability. Maybe that's the best thing for her. Her job is easy, but she has to deal with irate customers and that sometimes brings her stress. As she walks in, her supervisor, Karen, is waiting by the badge clock. She motions for Anika to follow her.

"Anika your aux score is too high. You're off the phone too much," Karen said.

"I drink a lot of water and I have to pee a lot. And I just had surgery," Anika said.

"That has nothing to do with your aux time being high. I'm going to write you up today. If you don't improve your aux time I will have to let you go," Karen said. Anika begins to cry.

"I can't believe you would insult me like this. I got yeast infections because I was holding in my pee. If I have to take a break I should be able to without any problems. I can't believe you're doing this to me," Anika said. Anika signed the document, but was so upset she could not continue to work. She left the building never to return. She didn't even question herself. She headed straight to the disability office to apply. If she had been taking her medication every day she would have been able to handle herself better. She wouldn't have lost her job. She had gone too long without it.

They gave her a form to fill out and she is expected to remember each time she was hospitalized. She got a note from her doctor saying that she is permanently disabled and cannot work, and included that in her file. A person from Social Security Disability called her the following week.

"I understand you want to apply for disability, is that correct?" the specialist asked.

"Yes, I do. I can't work anymore. It's too much stress. I have a mental disorder," Anika said.

"Do you happen to know when you are starting to have an episode?" The specialist asked.

"Yes. I see faces in the sheets and I get migraine head-aches every day," Anika said.

"I'm going to grant you your disability. Most people get denied their first attempt, but I'm positive that you need it," the specialist said.

"Yes, I do. Thank you so much." Anika began receiving disability one week after that conversation. She began receiving nine hundred thirty-five dollars per month in addition to paying for her Medicare. Anika could not believe it. Now she doesn't have to worry about losing her mind again. She has medication that has taken away those annoying voices, no job to stress her out and medical coverage.

CHAP T E R 1 5

Mosi is excited. He had decided to buy his first house. Anika is curious as to why he's not waiting until their marriage to buy this house. He rushes Anika to get ready. They have to pick out the interior and exterior of the house. This is the fun part for Mosi. They're going to build the house from the ground up. The blue print shows a kitchen, a large living room, 5 bedrooms, and 2 bathrooms.

"First, we're going to pick out the type of ceiling you want. You have your choice of a two feet by two feet Coffer white lay-in tile, or the Stucco Pro Revealed Edge tile, or the traditional Bermuda bronze lay in tile," the designer said.

"What do you think Anika?" Mosi asked. Anika walks away.

"What does it matter what I think? This is going to be your house. You don't even see me in it," Anika said.

"I do see you in it Anika. I see you handing me a beer and inviting over your friends," Mosi said.

Anika receives a call from Rachel. She rushes over to her apartment where a party is being held. Anika barely makes it into Rachel's door before she vomits onto the ground. Rachel helps her in. She suspects Anika is pregnant so she drives to the nearest store and buys a pregnancy test. Sure enough Anika is pregnant. Anika drives over to Mosi's house. Mosi is outside cooking fish on the grill. Anika picks up the tile sample from Mosi's future house.

"Are you ready for this," Anika asked.

"What's going on?" Mosi said.

"I'm pregnant Mosi," Anika said. Mosi takes the pregnancy test.

"Things are gonna get worse," Mosi said.

"What do you mean it's gonna get worse?" Anika questions.

"Our relationship, our relationship is going to get worse," Mosi said. Anika folds her arms boldly.

"But we're going to get married right?" Anika asked.

"Sometimes I want to get married, sometimes I don't," Mosi said.

"Is that why you never set a date?" Anika questioned. "Maybe we shouldn't be married right now Anika. Maybe we should wait longer," Mosi said.

"Don't do this to me Mosi!" Anika screams at the top of her lungs. She picks up her purse to head for the door. "Where are you going?" Mosi asked.

"I'm going back to Rachel's. I'll see you later," Anika said. Anika wanted to forget about the relationship. She wanted to just be by herself. She called Mosi once and he didn't answer so she called him three more times and he finally picked up.

"Mosi we should talk," Anika said.

"Ok, I'm going to make a quick stop and I'll call you later," Mosi said. Mosi stops at his friend's house to buy more marijuana. He stays over there until 4am. Anika calls him nine times, but his phone is on silent and he doesn't hear it ring. Mosi finally places his phone to normal before heading to bed.

"Where were you Mosi?" Anika questioned.

"I had to make a stop," Mosi said.

"A stop where?" Anika questioned.

"At my friend's house," Mosi said.

"Why you didn't answer your phone?" Anika questioned."It was on silent," Mosi said.

"You are cheating on me Mosi?" Anika asked.

"No, Anika," Mosi said.

"It's over," Anika said.

"Anika. Nobody's cheating on you," Mosi said.

Anika begins to get cramps in her stomach.

"Oh God," Anika said.

"Anika, are you alright?" Mosi asked.

Anika hangs up the phone and heads to the bathroom. She wipes herself with toilet tissue and sees blood. Clumps of blood began to leave her body. Her periods are usually heavy but this time it's different. She's not used to clumps of blood. Anika puts on a pad and then heads over to the emergency room. The doctors examine her and tell her she had a miscarriage. A flood of tears falls from her eyes. She sends Mosi a text to give him the news. He is a little relieved. She texted him once more. 'We should get back together. I miss you already.' He sends her a text back. 'No, I don't think that's a good idea. It's been over.' Anika's eye lids swells up with tears once again.

CHAPTER 16

Five years have passed and Anika and Mosi are still apart; she dreams of him often. She feels she should have tried harder to get him back. No other man has been able to take the place of Mosi, sexually or mentally. Mosi was her first love and he always kept her calm. Will she ever find the one? She could have sworn Mosi was the one.

"Maybe I should try to get in contact with him," Anika thinks.

Anika dials his number and it's disconnected. The only contact she has is Ms. Sultan. She gets up enough courage to give her a call.

"Who is this?" Ms. Sultan asked.

"It's Anika. I can't stop dreaming about Mosi. I think we should get back together," Anika said.

"Mosi doesn't want you," Ms. Sultan said.

"Is he married? Does he have any kids? I miss him." Anika said.

"No, he's not married. He hangs around his friends all day. He doesn't have time for a woman. I'm sorry to tell you this Anika, but you're not the one. You and he should have never been together," Ms. Sultan said.

Anika slams the phone down picks it back up and calls Rachel.

"How can I find Mosi? I need closure," Anika said.

"Look him up," Rachel said.

"Can you do it for me?" Anika asked.

"Sure," Rachel said. Rachel goes to her computer and pulls up a database to search for Mosi. She finds him in one minute.

"I found him. Write him a letter," Rachel said.

Anika knows she's a great writer. She hopes her letter is effective enough to cause Mosi to contact her. She begins to write, "Dear Mosi, It's been five years since we've spoken and it's really affecting me. I dream about you all the time. I've tried dating other men, I still dream about you and I don't know why. Maybe I didn't try hard enough to keep you. We were like Romeo and Juliet. I didn't know then what I know now and that's love is supposed to last forever. We should have never given up on our relationship. I've been taking my medication for five years now and I have not had a relapse. The doctors are giving me a different diagnosis. Some say I'm paranoid schizophrenic and some say I'm schizoaffective bipolar type. No one knows. Every time I had a nervous breakdown I had drugs in my system. Not because I do drugs, but because people around me did drugs. I've often wondered if you were married or had any kids? Maybe if we starting talking again the dreams will stop. At that point, maybe I can move on or maybe we can try to make it work one more time. I'm still in love with you and no other man has ever come close to pleasing me the way you did, sexually and emotionally. We should have gotten married. I think back to our college days when Mary told me you would cheat on me. That made me paranoid and ever since then I couldn't trust you. I wonder if we would have worked out if she didn't tell me that.

DON'T CALL ME CRAZY! AGAIN

Remember when we broke up and you wrote a letter to me and I got back with you. Well, that's what I'm doing to you. I'm writing you a letter in the hopes that you'll call me. Even if we don't get back together, I want us to talk so I can get some closure. The dreams just won't stop. I finished writing the book of fiction that was inspired by my true story and I'm doing really well. I'm giving lectures now and I was written up in the Florida Sentinel, the St. Pete bulletin, and N Touch News, and I wrote a movie about my book. I know I'm going to become famous. You told me you would never get married if you didn't marry me. I hope that is true, give me a call 555-4535." Anika waited weeks for a phone call, but got nothing. She would check her mail every day, but never got a letter from Mosi. He has moved on without her. She needs a man in her life. She won't be paranoid this time. She will be able to trust him. She's taking her medication and she is now stable. Anika waited weeks for a phone call, but got nothing. She would check her mail every day, but never got a letter from Mosi. He has moved on without her. She needs a man in her life. She won't be paranoid this time. She will be able to trust him. She's taking her medication and she is now stable.

115

CHAPTER 17

Anika prepares to do a speech for the Saint Petersburg Islamic center. She practices for hours. The next morning she arrives at the center ten minutes late. The Imam begins rushing her to get started. There's an audience of ten people. Two of her Facebook friends showed up. Anika sets up the camera, passes out flyers, and begins her speech.

"Hello, how is everyone doing? I'm Anika Muhammad and I inspire people to live out their dreams regardless of their disability. I believe everyone in here should be able to enhance their life, spiritually, mentally, and financially. Raise your hand if you agree that your life should be enhanced. I studied Psychology and Business at the University of South FL for five years and I received my BA degree in Psychology. All my life I considered myself normal. I never had any disciplinary problems in school and I made good grades. So when the doctors diagnosed me with the most debilitating mental disorder known in mental health, I denied it. I questioned their expertise. How could you go twenty-eight years of your life with no problems and then be diagnosed with a mental disorder? Later I learned there were warning signs. I have slurred speech, I have a family history of mental illness, and when I was eight years old I could hear music in my head. My mom told me that everyone could hear music in their head so I thought that meant that you could hear music in your head like the radio is playing. So I concentrated hard and I heard my favorite artist's songs in my head and I thought that was so amazing. I had no idea it had anything to do with mental illness.

You may wonder what could be so traumatic that I would develop a mental disorder. Well, I went through what many people go through, abuse as a child, and the loss of a job. I had a lot going on at one time with planning to be married while trying to find a job. I kept getting sicker and sicker. I saw faces everywhere. There were faces in the sheets, faces in the walls, faces in the rugs. And me having a BA degree in Psychology, I knew this was a warning sign of mental illness, but I still didn't put two and two together and say I have a mental problem. One day I was at my fiancé's house and I said now what if I could hear music again in my head like when I was eight years old. So I concentrated hard and I heard Tupac's song, "All eyes on me," in my head and I thought that was so amazing. One day I was watching TV and everything was about me. My fiancé saw that I was acting weird and he called my mom and she told him to bring to the hospital. On the way there I began receiving revelations and visions; some were from God, but some were due to my mental illness. Once I arrived at the hospital the doctors sat me down and said that I have paranoid schizophrenia and I was like, 'woah, no way.' They also said that I have obsessive-compulsive disorder, and anxiety. I insisted that I was normal and normal people don't get mental illnesses. So I refused to take the medicine and I was hospitalized again. Now I knew that you have to take your medication for at least three to six months when you have a nervous breakdown to balance the chemicals in your brain so I took the medication for a few months. I had a good paying job and I didn't want to lose it. I had a hard time waking up for work because the medicine was so strong, so I stopped taking it. Two years went by and everything was fine, but sometime after that I started seeing faces again and I started getting migraine headaches every day for six months and was hospitalized shortly thereafter. Again, the doctors sat me down and told me that I have paranoid schizophrenia. I was in a constant state of denial, refusing to take my medicine and as a result was hospitalized three more times. My fiancé got sick of me relapsing and took a picture of me at my worst. I looked at that picture and my hair was in disarray, my eyes were bulging out, I was crying. I remember thinking that this is what I see in those textbooks. I said, 'I am sick, I do need help.' I finally got enough courage to go to the pharmacy to get the medication. The pharmacy tech was staring at me like I was a lunatic and the pharmacist saw this and ran from behind the counter and held my hand and I started crying. He said, "There's nothing wrong with taking medication. Some people take medication for diabetes, heart problems. Take your medication and you'll be fine." So it's been five years now and I've been taking my medication every day and I have not had a relapse. There are benefits to taking your medication. I've been able to get my first book published and it didn't cost me a thing. It's a work of fiction inspired by my true story. If you feel that you need medication and you don't have insurance dial 211 and they will help you find a doctor that will see you. And if you feel like you're going to have a breakdown go straight to the emergency room. Don't wait to set up an appointment with a doctor. My book is more than a romance, it's about more than mental illness. It teaches people how to live out their dreams regardless of their disabilities. Raise your hand if you have dreams or goals. Some people here have reached their dreams and there are others that still have big dreams.

I've learned from Psychology the fastest way to reach your dreams is to change yourself. I heard a quote from Biggy and Puffy, 'you can't change the world until you change yourself.' I've learned through reading and overcoming trials and tribulations. It's helped me reach my goals and in my book I teach those things to you, my readers. For example, I tell you in my book to find something you love to do and would do for free and work on that talent. Even if you get bored, continue perfecting that talent and then read books and search the Internet for ways you can make a living by living your dreams. And I tell you, don't go running telling everyone about your dreams. Ninety percent of Americans hate their jobs and if you tell them your dreams they will tell you not to pursue it. They will tell you that you won't make it because they are insecure and they never pursued their dreams. Oprah said, 'True courage is becoming the person you dream to be.' I want to enhance your life so please stop by the autograph table and I will personally sign your book. Are there any questions?"

"Are schizophrenics violent?"

"Sixty percent of Americans think schizophrenics are violent but that is just not true for most of us. The majority of schizophrenics are not violent unless there are drugs or alcohol involved. I, myself, never did drugs, but years ago one of my friends was putting cocaine in my system and I'm told that when I was in the hospital I was kicking at people's feet, but I never hit anyone. I had a strong family support system."

"How many personalities do you have?"

"None. Schizophrenia and split personality disorder are two totally different disorders," Anika said.

"How many people experience schizophrenia?"

"One percent of Americans," Anika said.

"How many people experience mental illness?"

"Fifty seven million Americans a year will experience a mental disorder," Anika said.

"How many of those receive treatment?"

"Only 13% of Americans receive treatment, which is entirely too low. That's why I'm trying my best to bring the word out about mental illness. Are there any other questions?" No one raises their hand.

"Thank you for coming out. Please visit the autograph table and buy a copy of my book. Thank you."

People rush over to the autograph table and purchased books from Anika. Anika loves to give speeches. She doesn't get nervous at all. There was a reporter in the audience and he pulled Anika to the side to ask questions. He invited her to a book signing at a support group where they talk about ways to improve themselves. He wants to put her in the number one newspaper in the city for African Americans. Anika feels like her dreams are coming true.

After the speech Anika searches her medicine cabinet for her medications, but can't find any. She has run out. She starts to think, *"What if I lose my mind again?"* And the moment she thought that, she started feeling like she would lose her mind. It felt like her world was falling at her feet. Two days went by and she could not sleep. She would toss and turn and get up several times to use the bathroom. She knew she would not have a relapse because she had been on medication for five years. She has experienced a relapse and knows the warning signs. She would have racing thoughts and she would see faces in the sheets. This was different. This felt like a panic attack. After two days of no sleep, she was finally able to see her nurse practitioner.

"How are you doing Anika?" Becky asked.

"I think I'm experiencing panic attacks," Anika said.

"What are you experiencing?" Becky asked.

"It feels like I'm going to lose my mind."

"You can't talk yourself out of that?" Becky asked.

"Sometimes I can but then it comes back," Anika said.

"When you say you're going to lose control, do you mean you're angry?" Becky asked.

"No, I'm not angry," Anika said.

"Ok, I'm going to increase your Clomipramine. That should help," Becky said.

CHAPTER 18

A week goes by and Anika picks up the newspaper. The article is beautiful. She drives back home to her mother's house to show her the good news. She reads the article out loud, "On Saturday, November 18, 2011 from 12 noon to 1pm, author Anika Muhammad will present a free presentation and reading from her published novel. 'I wrote my book to end the stigma of mental illness and to help the community grow mentally, spiritually, and financially. It took me two years to get my books into the public library system. I'm reaching all my goals and I want to help the community reach all of their goals.' Fifty-seven million Americans will suffer from a mental disorder this year and only 13% of them will seek treatment. Thirty thousand lives are lost each year because people are afraid to seek help. They're afraid to be labeled as crazy." Anika Muhammad received her BA in Psychology and has been diagnosed with the most debilitating mental illness known in mental health, paranoid schizophrenia, and for a long time refused to take medication. I always saw myself as normal and I thought that normal people don't get mental illnesses. I want to reach out to the African American community."

"That's a great article. You're actually living your dreams. I can't wait until the book reading," Ms. Muhammad said.

A week went by and as Anika began driving to the book signing in Tampa, she started feeling like she would lose her mind again. Increasing the medication didn't work. She places the palm of her hands against her head. The attacks were getting worse. She began to have uncontrollable movement in her lips and when she tried to speak it was slurred. Anika will have to give her speech while experiencing a panic attack. When she talks, she says little. She wants to get the speech out the way. Something that used to be fun for her is now a strain.

Anika finishes her speech and begins signing autographs. No one noticed that she was experiencing this attack. The organizer of the support group began to speak. She is a beautiful African American in her late forty's. She wears her hair straight and permed. She works alongside Dr. Steward who is a retired clinical psychotherapist. He is an older man in his eighties and dresses, modest for a doctor.

"Our topic for today is what do you want to change about yourself?" Sophia said.

"I wish I was more positive," Anika said.

"So you're a negative person," Dr. Steward said.

"No, I wouldn't call myself negative," Anika said.

"Well, until you can acknowledge your problem, you can't change. We are all fucked up and we have to learn how to unfuck ourselves," Dr. Steward said.

"I don't think everyone is fucked up. I think some people have it together," Anika said.

"Name one person," Dr. Steward said.

"I know some people, but I don't want to share their business," Anika said.

"So what else do you want to change?" Dr. Steward said.

"I want a man in my life," Anika said.

"Well, what is it you want in a man?" Dr. Steward asked.

"I want someone that is financially successful, and someone faithful," Anika said.

"You're a gold digger. You didn't say you want a man who knows God, you said you want a man financially stable," An obese older man said.

"I'm not a gold digger. There's nothing wrong with a woman wanting a man to take care of her. And besides, I'm not materialistic. I just want a man that can help me further my career. There's nothing wrong with that," Anika said. "What's in your bank account?" Simon said.

"That's none of your business!" Anika said.

"What you should do is start having sex with different men. That would help you. Just start having sex. I want to buy one of your books and I want you to sign it, you can have sex with me anytime and here's my number," Simon said.

"I'm not writing that. What if your wife finds it?" Anika asked. "If that's what he wants you to write in his book, then that's what you should write in his book," Dr. Steward said.

"I don't agree. She doesn't have to write that," Attiq said.

"If she wants that money she gone have to sign it that way," Dr. Steward said.

"You can buy a book, but I'm not signing that," Anika said. Simon handed Anika money for the book and Anika signed it, reach for the stars. Thank you for your support. Simon throws Anika's book at her face.

"How are you gone tell me to reach for the stars?! I'm an old man and I've already accomplished my dreams," Simon said. Anika says nothing and begins to pack up her books. Attiq follows her. Attiq is an older Muslim in his late forties with a slender build and is a wealthy man. Word has it that he put all of his children through college and bought them all houses, but he has a reputation for being cheap when it comes to treating the woman in his life. He is single. He was married six times, but the marriages didn't work out.

"Let me carry those books for you. Are you enjoying the people in the support group?" Attiq asked.

"No, I'm not. This was my first time coming," Anika said.

"Are you Muslim?" Attiq asked.

"Yes, I am," Anika said.

"Do you mind if I call you sometime?" Attiq asked. "As a matter of fact, I don't mind." Anika said. She had heard the rumors about him being a cheap man, but she wasn't going to allow gossip to interfere with what could potentially be a good thing. Gossip is just that, gossip. A week later she meets up with him at McDonalds.

"Are you hungry? Do you want something to eat?" Attiq asked.

"No, not at all," Anika said.

"You're so beautiful. Tell me why you're single?" Attiq asked.

"I don't know, I guess I haven't found the right one yet. My last boyfriend turned out to be gay. I don't hold it against him. I think he was molested as a child. For other reasons, though, I was never able to trust him.

He was faithful to me at first, but in the end he cheated on me. So I guess we're both at fault," Anika said.

"No, he was at fault. He should have never cheated. Sometimes children grow up without a father and they only have their mother and sisters to look up to. They start imitating their behavior. They start dressing like her, wearing her wigs, and then they become gay. Every man has a natural instinct to be a man. And they ignore that instinct and become a transvestite. God didn't create gays. God doesn't make mistakes. I would say for you to read the Quran and then you will see the truth," Attiq said.

"I don't mean to change the subject, but I can't stop noticing how beautiful you are. It will benefit me just to be with you even if we don't have sex, but of course, we can," Attiq said.

"I'm not going to have sex with anyone until I fall in love," Anika said.

"When was the last time you had sex?" Attiq asked.

"Five years ago," Anika said.

"Well, if you had sex then you can have sex now," Attiq"It won't be anytime soon," Anika said.

"I want you to promise me something. Promise me that you won't tell anyone that we're seeing each other. I have enemies and they may try to break us up," Attiq said.

"Are you seeing anybody?" Anika asked.

"No, I'm not dating anyone," Attiq said.

"Well, if you're trying to keep us a secret, then it sounds to me that you're seeing someone and you don't want them to know," Anika said.

"No, it's not that. I just don't want anyone in my business," Attiq said.

"Ok, we'll see how it goes," Anika said.

"It's close to Ramadan. During Ramadan I won't get close to you at all because I'll be fasting and we're not supposed to have sex during the day. But I still want to see you. I want you to come to Tampa to my Masjid," Attiq said.

"I need help with gas," Anika said.

"Will five dollars help?" Attiq said.

"No. It cost me 10 dollars to drive to Tampa," Anika said.

"I'm going to get the Muslims to give you a little help during Ramadan," Attiq said. Anika couldn't help but think, *"What about now? I need help now,"* but she remained quiet.

"Let me walk you to your car. Can I have a kiss?" Attiq asked. "No. You know a woman doesn't kiss on the first date," Anika said.

"This is not a date. We're just friends," Attiq said.

"Well, if we're just friends why are you trying to kiss me?" Anika asked. Attiq just smiled and shut the door for her and Anika drove away.

CHAP T E R 1 9

Anika meets with her nurse practitioner again.

"So is the medicine working?" Becky asked.

"No, I'm still having these attacks," Anika said.

"Maybe it's a good idea for you to see a counselor. I'm going to introduce you to Bettie. Follow me," Becky said. Bettie is an older woman in her fifties. She dresses in cheap garments. The mental health field doesn't pay very well.

"So Anika how can I help you?" Bettie asked.

"I'm getting these attacks. I don't know if they're panic attacks or not, but twice a week I feel like I'm going to lose my mind. All I do is think about losing control and I start having these attacks where I begin having uncontrollable lip movement and slurred speech. It's like I'm doing it to myself. I was molested when I was young and I never received counseling, so I think the attacks are from the molestation," Anika said.

"No the molestation doesn't have anything to do with these attacks. This is a compulsive behavior from your obsessive compulsive disorder," Bettie said. Anika begins to think to herself, *"Why do I need counseling then?"*

"Do you ever feel any other type of anxiety?" Bettie asked.

"When I'm a passenger in a car and we go over a hump in the road, I get a gust of anxiety then," Anika said.

"Now that could be from the molestation. We can talk more about that next time. Come back in a week," Bettie said.

Anika left that building and headed straight for a psychotherapist office. She needs some type of counseling or medication that can get rid of her panic attacks. The doctor saw her immediately. She didn't even have to set an appointment.

"What brings you in today?" Dr. Sanders asked. "I'm getting these attacks. It feels like I'm going to lose my mind. I get them twice a week and some days I stay up for two days straight with the attack. Am I having a panic attack?" Anika asked.

"You're having an anxiety attack. What medications are you on?" Dr. Sanders asked. "75 mg of Clomipramine and 160 mg of Geodon," Anika said.

"There is nothing for the anxiety? You need medication for the anxiety. I'm going to prescribe .5mg of Clonazepam that you will take it one hour before you go to bed. Is there anything else you need help with?" Sanders asked.

"I want you to give me a diagnosis. I was diagnosed with paranoid schizophrenia when I was first hospitalized and now the doctors are trying to change my diagnosis," Anika said. "What did you experience during your breakdown?" Sanders asked.

"I was paranoid that my boyfriend was cheating on me and I thought that when we had sex he had cameras up. I hallucinated and I thought I saw God," Anika said.

"I would diagnose you with schizoaffective bipolar type because of the anxiety. You don't have paranoid schizophrenia," Sanders said.

"Will they take away my disability?" Anika asked.

"No, because the two disorders are too similar. You're going to need disability until maybe your book does well," Sanders said.

"You know about my book?" Anika questioned.

"Yes, I read about it in the paper. You were in the top newspaper in Saint Petersburg," Sanders said.

"I also need help finding a part-time job. Do you know anyone that's hiring?" Anika asked. Sanders hands Anika a paper with an address listed on it.

"Go here. They accept people who are on disability and you only have to work part time. They will interview you on the spot," Sanders said. Anika rushed right over to this company. There were fifty people in the waiting room asking for applications.

"I'll never get this job," Anika thought. She then remembered that she has to begin thinking more positive, so she decided to wait to be called in for an interview. An hour goes by before she hears her name called by the recruiter. He was a short man with a thick mustache and glasses. He looks down at Anika's application.

"So tell me about your experience in customer service?" Richard asked.

"I have several years of experience in a call center environment. We would take incoming calls from credit card holders wanting to know about their balance and next payment due. It was a pretty easy job," Anika said.

"So how did you deal with irate customers?" Richard asked.

"I would listen without interruption and let them vent and if that didn't work I would put the call on hold for thirty seconds to give them time to cool down. That usually worked. But I understand with this type of job we wouldn't be able to place them on hold," Anika said. "That's correct. How do you connect with your customers?" Richard asked.

"By acknowledging their birthdays and anniversaries," Anika said.

"In this job, there's a lot of micromanaging. Would that bother you?" Richard asked.

"No, not at all. In my last customer service job we were monitored a lot and that didn't bother me at all. I don't see it as micromanaging. I think micromanaging is when you walk up and down the aisles waiting for someone to make a mistake and then you jump on them," Anika said.

"In this job a month may go by and you will have no work. How can you deal with that?" Richard asked.

"I will just save my money so I'll have money during the slow times," Anika said. "Our pay is $9.75 per hour. Would that be ok?" Richard asked.

"Yes," Anika said.

"Ok then you can start in a month. I'm going to do a background check and if that goes through ok, you got the job," Richard said.

"Thank you. Thank you so much". This was the happiest time in Anika's life. She got everything she wanted; disability, and a good paying part- time job. Now all she needs is a man. She calls up her new friend Attiq.

"I can't believe it! I got a job, I got my disability, and my book. Now all I need to do is find the love of my life," Anika said.

"Well, you just broke my heart because I thought I was the one. You built me up and then let me right back down," Attiq said.

"I'm sorry," Anika said.

"Are you coming to see me today? I'll have some gas money for you," Attiq said.

"Yes, but first I'm going to go to lunch with some friends. I'll call you later," Anika said. Anika drives across the bridge for lunch and she started experiencing an anxiety attack again. She had medicine, but she couldn't take it until nighttime. She has to struggle with anxiety for another day. When she begins talking to her group of friends the anxiety went away.

"The topic for today is why do women cheat?" Dr. Stewart said.

"Who do you think cheats more doctor? Men or women?" Brian asked.

"I think it's about the same, but I think women are sneakier than men. Raise your hand if you have ever cheated on your lover?" Dr. Stewart asked. There were four women in the room and six men. Every last man raised his hand, but none of the woman raised their hand.

"Now you see what we got here. The men will be more honest and admit their mistakes while the woman are remaining quiet," Dr. Stewart said.

"It all depends on how you define cheating. If it's dating someone else while you're in a relationship then yes I've cheated, but if it's having sex with two people at the same time then no I haven't cheated," Anika said.

"No, we're not talking about dating. We're talking about having sex with another man," Dr. Stewart said.

"Then no, I never cheated," Anika said.

"I don't believe you. In your book you stated that you cheated," Brian said.

"My book is fictional and in my book I said the character fooled around with another man, but they never had sex," Anika said.

"Well, I think that's cheating," Brian said.

"Well, I agree with you," Anika said.

"Now let's not get off the topic. The topic is why do women cheat?" Dr. Steward said.

"Why did you cheat Anika?" Brian asked.

"For revenge, but that was a long time ago I wouldn't do that now," Anika said.

"How long ago?" Brian asked. Anika didn't say a word she just looked at him.

"Woman cheat because they can get away with it. They're a lot sneakier than man," Dr. Stewart said.

Brian begins to laugh. "I sure agree with that," Brian said.

Anika packs up her books to leave. She has to head towards the Masjid to see Attiq. She has her head covered in a black and gold scarf and a long sleeved blouse and black pants to match. She doesn't particularly care to dress like this, but in the company of Muslims she feels it's only respectful. Her mother taught her that when God says to cover thy self in public he means to be a wholesome good woman in public; it doesn't necessarily mean you have to cover your entire body up. Anika is used to dressing sexy with her arms and legs showing. She makes it to the Masjid and Attiq is at the front door to greet her. He doesn't want anyone to know that they're dating so he doesn't show any affection. Anika sits across from the men and Attiq approaches her.

"I think some more women are coming to the Masjid; do you want to sit over there in the corner where the women usually sits?" Attiq asked.

"No, I'm fine right here," Anika said. Anika notices the embarrassment on Attiq's face and she stands to move.

"Thank you. I really appreciate it," Attiq said. Anika walks over to the small corner and sits, waiting for the other woman to enter. The Masjid is a small business building overlooking the lake. It's Ramadan so everyone is fasting. The Imam in the Masjid hands out watermelon for everyone to eat before their breakfast. The Imam called for prayer and Anika stood along with everyone else. Everyone brings their heads to the floor to give Allah praise. When the prayer is over they eat. The service is over and Anika expects Attiq to walk her to the car but he doesn't. He asked another man to walk her to the car.

She thought that was going too far. Anika almost escaped the anxiety attacks, but as soon as she gets into her car to drive back to Saint Petersburg, the panic attacks start. She places her hands against her temples and the car begins to swerve. She looks in her rear view mirror and she sees the lights from a police car flashing. She pulls over to the side of the road.

"Your car is swerving. Are you on any medication?" The policeman asked.

"I am, but I can't take it until this evening. I'll be okay," Anika said as she smiled, hoping he wouldn't think she was unfit to drive.

"What's your mental illness?" The policeman asked.

"I have paranoid schizophrenia and I was beginning to have a panic attack," Anika said. Anika begins to breathe heavily.

"Ok, please drive safe," the policeman said. And he let her go. She continues to drive home while experiencing the anxiety attacks. She watches the road more carefully because she becomes paranoid about getting into a car accident. She makes it home at 9pm and takes her new medication right away. She lies down and immediately falls asleep. The medicine doesn't stop the attacks, but it does stop her from staying awake for two days so that is a big improvement.

CHAP T E R 2 0

A month goes by and Ramadan is over. Now Attiq feels like he can conquer sex from Anika. It's only been a month and Attiq claims he's in love with her, but Anika didn't believe it so she asked God before she went to sleep, "Is Attiq the one?" And when she awoken she realized that she had received the message that Attiq is telling her he is in love with her so he can have sex with her. This made Anika even more careful. Attiq invites her to a Muslims house to celebrate the end of Ramadan. They meet at a gas station and he told her to follow him to his house because he needed to change clothes. They both park their car in the parking lot and then Attiq approaches her.

"Why don't you come in for a minute?" Attiq said.

"No, I think I'll wait out here," Anika said.

"Well, I'm disappointed in you. I thought we'd spend some time together at my house before we go to the Muslim's house," Attiq said.

"No, I'm going to stay right here," Anika said Attiq gives her a disappointed frown and walks inside his house to change. He steps out and gets into his car and Anika follows him to the Muslims house. They are not allowed to sit together. Anika goes inside the house with the women while Attiq stays outside with the men. She doesn't understand the purpose of them going to an event together if they can't even spend time together, but she remembers the Arabic traditions and remains inside the house with the woman. She hands out flyers of her book to the women sitting waiting for prayer.

"Is this a true story?" Aaliyah asked.

"It's inspired by a true story," Anika said. Aaliyah reads the back of the book.

"Have you been hospitalized before?" Aaliyah asked.

"Yes, six times," Anika said.

"Do you really know when you're about to lose control?" Aaliyah asked.

"I take my medication now. I haven't had a relapse in five years, but yes. I can tell before it happens," Anika said.

"I believe that a lot of people have a nervous breakdown at least once in their lives, but that doesn't mean you need to take medication. I was hospitalized ten years ago. I had a nervous breakdown, but I've been able to do fine without the medicine. Allah saved my life," Aaliyah said.

"I do believe in miracles that God gives to some people. But I need my medication. I would not be able to function without it," Anika said.

"So you believe you're crazy?" Aaliyah asked.

"No, not crazy... gifted. Many people have to take medication for the rest of their lives for physical problems. If they're not crazy then neither am I," Anika said.

They pray, eat, and then leave. Anika follows Attiq to his house again and he goes inside to change his clothes. He finishes and walks up to Anika's car.

"It's still early; can we go to the movies?" Anika asked.

"No. I have been sitting all day. I think I want to go to the beach and talk, follow me," Attiq said. Anika follows Attiq as he pulls up into a hotel parking lot. She wonders why they are even there.

"Come sit in the car with me Anika," Attiq said.

"Why are we at a hotel?" Anika asked.

"I was hoping I could talk you into sleeping with me," Attiq said.

"No," Anika said.

"Leave your car here. I want you to ride with me. Let's go to the beach," Attiq said. He parks his car on the beach sand and they both walk hand in hand down the strip. Anika stops at an ice scream shop.

"Can I get some ice cream?" Anika asked.

"No. I don't have my wallet on me," Attiq said.

"Then what if I would have agreed to have sex with you in the hotel? How would you have paid for the hotel?" Anika said.

"I would of gone back home and got my wallet," Attiq said. Anika opens her purse and takes out her ATM card. She has seven dollars left to buy some ice scream. She doesn't have enough to buy two ice cream cones so she buys one and shares it with Attiq. They continue walking down the strip.

"Why didn't you come into my house with me? You really disappointed me," Attiq said.

"I'm not ready for sex, so I'm not going to go into your house," Anika said."You don't trust me do you?" Attiq said.

"Well, it's obvious you were trying to get some sex from me and I told you already I'm not ready, so why would you try me?" Anika said.

138

"Why don't you want to please me?" Attiq asked.

"Well, you didn't please me either. You didn't take me to the movies. Someone must have hurt you really bad because you don't seem to want to spend any money on women," Anika said.

"What if I do spend money and the relationship doesn't work?" Attiq asked.

"Then you enjoy the time that you spent with the woman," Anika said.

"I want you to marry me, but I don't want you to tell anyone. We can get married by my Imam the Muslim way. We don't have to sign any court room papers?" Attiq said.

"The most special day for a woman is her wedding day. I wouldn't keep that a secret," Anika said.

"You just have to trust me. Fifty percent of marriages end in divorce because everyone is in your business. I'm going to ask you to do a lot of things you're not going to understand. You're just going to have to do them. Like for example, you're going to have to change the way you dress. A Muslim sister shouldn't have her stuff out like that," Attiq said.

"There's nothing wrong with the way I dress," Anika said.

"How do you know?" Attiq said.

"I talk to God all the time before I go to bed. I'll ask him a question and when I wake up I'll have the answer. So you know I'm a Muslim woman and Muslim women are not supposed to have sex before marriage, so why do you want me to dress appropriately, but you are trying to have sex with me?" Anika said.

"You did it before you can do it again," Attiq said.

"Well, I personally don't believe you have to be married to have sex, but I know that many Imam's preach that fornication is wrong and you follow what those Imam's say so you shouldn't be trying to get sex from me," Anika said.

"That's why I said we can get married by my Imam and that way we don't have to feel guilty about having sex. And if we last for six months with no problems, then we can go to the courts to get married," Attiq said.

"No, I don't think so," Anika said.

"So what do you want to do now?" Attiq asked.

"I want to go home," Anika said. Attiq drives her back to the hotel, she gets into her car and drives off. She didn't call him for a week, so he called her.

"So why aren't you calling me? You must not like me," Attiq said.

"I like you, but I feel like you're holding back. Someone hurt you and you're taking it out on me," Anika said.

"Come with me to a Muslim event tomorrow morning," Attiq said.

"I can't. I'm going to Arabic class tomorrow," Anika said.

"You know you really disappointed me," Attiq said.

"I'll call you tomorrow," Anika said. The next morning Anika woke up late and missed her Arabic class so she called Attiq and he told her to meet him at a gas station.

He had a gift to give her for skipping her class. They meet at the gas station and Anika followed him to his house. He had a dress for her to try on and wanted her to get out of the car. She fell for his trick.

"Try the dress on. Get undressed in front of me, I want to see you," Attiq said. Anika was a little hesitant and naïve and did as he said. She tried the dress on. It was a beautiful long red gown with a zipper in the back. She took the dress off and tried to put her clothes back on but Attiq told her to keep her clothes off. He walked her over to his bed and began kissing her neck. He then completely undressed and lay beside her in the nude."I'm going to get a condom," Attiq said.

"No, I'm not ready," Anika said.

"Well can you suck me," Attiq said.

"No, I'm not ready. I told you before that I wasn't ready," Anika said.

"Are you just going to leave me hanging?" Attiq asked. Anika remains quiet.

"Put on your clothes," Attiq said in disgust. Fearing his next words she hurried into the bathroom to put back on her clothes and Attiq followed her.

"Let me hit it from the back?" Attiq said.

"No," Anika said.

"Alright, I'm going to take a shower. Do you want to take a shower?" Attiq asked.

"No," Anika said. Anika got dressed and followed him to a different Muslims house. It was the same old thing she had to stay inside with the women while he hung outside with the men. When the event was over Anika followed him to the beach.

"Why did you just leave me hanging like that?" Attiq asked.

"You left yourself hanging. You knew I wasn't ready," Anika said.

"You should have had sex even if you weren't ready because I wanted it. If I tell you to fuck me in this car you should fuck me in this car," Attiq said.

"No, I don't think so. You don't value women; that's your problem," Anika said.

"Let me tell you a story so you can know about me. I invited this woman to spend time with me in Africa. She didn't have to pay a thing. I paid for the flight, the hotel, and the food. I took a shower and got undressed and I asked her to do the same. She must have spent an hour in that restroom and she came out fully clothed. I asked her what she was doing. And she said, "You didn't tell me I had to have sex with you." I paid for the first plane flight out of there. See, I'm not that bad of a guy," Attiq said.

"I meet her two years after that and I found out that she was a prostitute. See I told you that story to let you know that I do value women," Attiq said.

"I think I want to go," Anika said. Anika got into her car and drove home. A week went by and she did not call him so he called her.

"Why haven't you called me? Tell me if you want to be just friends or do you want to make this relationship work?" Attiq asked.

"I just want to be friends, but you can call me if you'd like," Anika said.

"No, I'm not going to call you if you just want to be friends. Why do you hurt me like this?" Attiq said.

"I'm sorry," Anika said. A month went by and neither of them picked up the phone. He showed up one day where she and a group of her friends hang out, waited for her friends to leave, then walked over to Anika's car.

"Someone hurt you real bad and you won't spend a dime on a woman. That needs to change," Anika said.

"Maybe it has. Meet me somewhere, let's talk," Attiq said.

"No, I'm not going anywhere with you," Anika said and drove off.

CHAPTER 21

Anika meets up with her psychotherapist.

"So how is the medicine working for you?" Sanders asked.

"I'm still getting anxiety attacks but I go to sleep right away. I don't stay up for two days anymore," Anika said.

"Then the medicine is working. It may take some time to work fully. The more sleep you get, the better the medication will work. Tell yourself that you have been ok for five years and you're not going to have another relapse," Sanders said.

Anika prepares for her first day of work. She wears a casual black and white dress. It takes her forty minutes and twelve dollars to get to work. The company just hired on two-hundred new employees. Some work in the daytime and others work in the evening. Anika chooses to work in the evening. She waits in line to have her ID and social security card copied and the anxiety attacks begin. She looks down at her dress to make sure it's fitting correctly. Her mouth is moving uncontrollably and she hopes no one sees her. She does as the doctor suggests and tells herself she won't have a relapse, but that doesn't help. The anxiety attacks don't go away. The trainer trains for four hours and then puts everyone on the phone. Anika is experiencing severe slurred speech. She hopes that none of the clients recognize her slurred speech. One man said he couldn't understand her and he got off the phone but he had an accent so Anika thought it might be a language barrier. Anika stares at the clock hoping for eleven o'clock to arrive. She feels again like she's going to go out of her mind.

How can she help anyone overcome mental illness if she can't even overcome it? She drives home and the entire time she pays close attention to the road. She's terrified someone may pass a red light or not stop at a stop sign. She is paranoid. She makes it home and immediately takes her new medication. She lies in bed for two hours without sleep, tossing and turning thinking of the worst.

"What if someone in my family gets hurt? What if I can't fall asleep and I have to go to work like this," Anika thought. She can't control her negative thoughts. After two and a half hours of tossing and turning she finally goes to sleep. The next week she makes it over to her group of friends. She hands out her flyers and couldn't help but notice an older gentleman sitting by himself. She felt her self very attracted to him so she introduces herself.

"Hello, I'm Anika. I'm an author my book is called, 'The Truth Behind Closed Doors.' Here is a flyer. The book is doing well, but it could do much better," she said.

"If the book is doing so well, why are you handing out flyers?" the man asked.
This caught Anika off guard, but it might just be the, "in," she was looking for.

"It's expensive to hire a publicist; six thousand dollars," Anika said.

"It's nice to meet you. I'm Clifford. I may be able to help you come January," he said. Anika could not believe it. She wanted so desperately for someone to believe in her and help her pursue her dreams. Here is a man who didn't even know her and he was trying to help her out.

"He must be the one," Anika thought. Clifford is an older man in his fifty's. The perfect age for Anika because she doesn't want a young man that wants kids. Clifford is retired from his factory job and is still waiting for his pension.

Dr. Steward began the discussion and Anika took her seat.

"The topic for today is, 'Do as I say, but not as I do.' Many people will tell their kids not to lie, yet will turn right around and tell that same child to lie for them if some calls and they don't want to talk to them. 'Just tell them I'm not here.' I think we all at one time or another have been acting as a hypocrite," Dr. Steward said.

"Not me; I'm not a hypocrite," Anika said.

"Everyone is a hypocrite," Dr. Steward said.

"If I tell my child not to eat in the living room because he will make a mess and then I eat in the living room, I'm not being a hypocrite I'm just setting the rules because I know he will make a mess and I won't. I've learned from reading that when some- one is a certain type of person like a hypocrite they think that everyone is a hypocrite. You're a hypocrite not me," Anika said. Everyone remains quiet for a few seconds.

"You're crazy," Soulful said. Soulful is an attractive Afri- can American. He has a girlfriend, but cheats on her with many different women. He's had sex with more than two-hundred women. He believes that since he eats healthy, he's immune from getting a disease. He doesn't use protection. His girlfriend has no idea that he's cheating on her. They have been together for ten years without marriage and Soulful thinks of her as someone he lives with, but he doesn't consider her his girlfriend. Soulful doesn't believe in Aids. He thinks it's all made up.

DON'T CALL ME CRAZY! AGAIN

"When someone makes a judgment call about some-one they don't know they're really talking about themselves or someone close to them," Anika said. She should have remained quiet so that Soulful could have said what was really on his mind.

"You've been hospitalized more than me so that makes you crazy," Soulful said.

"So you've been hospitalized before?" Anika asked.

"No," Soulful said.

"But you said you've been hospitalized more than me. That means you have been hospitalized before," Anika said.

"How does that mean I've been hospitalized before? I said more than me meaning I've never been hospitalized. I don't think suffering from an anxiety attack makes you crazy," Soulful said.

"She is a writer and you did say more than me so that means you were hospitalized before. Anika would you date Soulful knowing he doesn't use condoms and he sleeps around?" Dr. Steward says. Anika takes a long pause.

"She probably has all already slept with him. That pause was too long," Gloria said.

"No, I wouldn't sleep with him. I use protection with every man I'm with. And I will do this until I'm married," Anika said.

"Are you attracted to me?" Soulful asked.

"I'm not going to answer that," Anika said.

"I think if you're attracted to someone you should say it," Soulful said.

"No, I'm not attracted to you and besides, you cheat. I want a faithful man," Anika said.

"All men cheat unless they're gay. I was at a club last night and a gay man felt on my arm. I yanked him up by his collar and told him not to ever touch me," Soulful said.

"You did the right thing. I hate gays, especially when they try to force their beliefs on you. You should have hit him," Simon said.

"Then he would have gotten arrested," Anika said.

"No, I think by putting him in his place I let everyone around there know I'm no faggot," Soulful said.

"I feel like you two are homophobic," Dr. Steward said.

"No, I'm not homophobic. That faggot shouldn't have put his hand on another man. That's all there is to it," Simon said.

"I'm ok with people being gay as long as they don't touch me. I'm going back up to that club tonight," Simon said.

"We should start laying down what's right and wrong and not be afraid to do it. Gays should not be together. I can show you in the bible that it's wrong, the preacher said."

"Ok everyone we're not going to talk about religion in here. We have Muslims, Baptist, and Catholics in here," Sophia said.

"Is there anyone that comes here that you're interested in?" Sophia asked.

"No," Anika said and Clifford almost fell out of his seat. Anika noticed it because she's very observant. She walks out to her car and Soulful follows. He opens the door for her.

"So are you attracted to me?" Soulful asked as he tries to feel on her leg. Anika stops him with the palm of her hand.

"No, I'm not attracted to you. And besides you have a girlfriend," Anika said.

"She's not my girlfriend," Soulful said.

"But you live with her. And you have kids by her. Does she know you cheat on her?" Anika asked.

"I'm not cheating. I can be with whomever I choose," Soulful said.
"Well, you don't believe in using condoms so I wouldn't be with you anyway," Anika said.

"Do you use condoms when you're having oral sex?" Soulful asked.

"No. It's difficult to catch Aids from oral sex so no I don't use condoms, but I do require anyone I sleep with to get tested first. And I always test myself once a year," Anika said.

"Well, we can have oral sex. I don't need to get tested. I got a disease one time and was cured of it so my body has built up an immune from diseases," Soulful said.

"No, we can't have any type of sex. I have to go. I'll see you later," Anika said. The next day Anika calls Sophia to ask her for Clifford's number. And she immediately gave him a call; she didn't want to mess up her opportunity to date him.

"Hello, this is Anika. We met yesterday," Anika said.

"I know who this is," Clifford said.

"I got your number from Sophia. I noticed you all most fell out of your chair when I said I wasn't interested in anyone. I just didn't want anyone in my business," Anika said.

"I was going to call you anyway," Clifford said.

"So are you dating anyone?" Anika asked.

"No, are you?" Clifford asked.

"No," Anika said.

"I was going to call you anyway, but just hadn't gotten around to it yet. So when do you want to go out? And what would you want to do?" Clifford said.

"How about the movies," Anika said.

"Ok, we can do that and then maybe you can spend some time at the salon. You can get your eyebrows arched… your toes done… Doesn't that sound good?" Clifford asked, melodically.

"Yes, it does," Anika said. The next week they meet at the Tyrone mall to see a movie. There were no good movie playing so they decided to walk the mall.

"Where do you want to get your toes done?" Clifford asked.

"There's only one store here that does it, follow me," Anika said. Anika sat in the massage chair while the nail tech placed her feet in the water. She felt so relaxed.

"Have you ever had a man get your toes done before?" Clifford asked.

"No, I haven't. I had a man offer, but I just never got around to it. This is nice. Thank you," Anika said.

"I'm going to love you like no other man has loved you before," Clifford said.

"Yes, I believe you're the one. I've never had a man care so much for me before and you don't pressure me for sex," Anika said.

"Now don't go comparing me to other guys," Clifford said.

"I'm not. You're nothing like those other guys. So tell me how old are you?" Anika asked.

"I'm old enough to be your father. Your mother is going to be like, What's this old man doing with my daughter?"

"No, she won't. My mother doesn't get into my business and besides, I like older men who are at least fifty because they're settled and already have children. I don't want any kids. I would be angry if a man got me pregnant," Anika said.

"Why is that? What's wrong with having a child?" Clifford asked.

"I want to be famous and having kids will just get in the way," Anika said.

"You could hire a nanny. You ever thought about that?" Clifford asked.

"I don't want to hunt for a babysitter. I just want to be able to get up and go," Anika said.

"Do you believe in abortion?" Clifford asked.

"No, I don't," Anika said.

"Well, we both agree that's not an option," Clifford said.

"No, it isn't," Anika said.

The nail tech begins to file Anika's toes. It's been a year since she had a pedicure. She thought she couldn't afford it. The nail tech takes Anika's feet out of the water and dries them off with a towel. She lotion's Anika's feet and legs and massages them. This is Anika's favorite part. Anika closes her eyes and inhales and then exhales.

"You know I want to be an actress. I have a photo shoot coming up this week," Anika said.

"I want to be there," Clifford said.

"Yes, you can come," Anika said.

"What color do you want?" The nail tech asked.

"Bright orange," Anika said. The nail tech paints her toes and sits her underneath the fan to dry her nails. Clifford hands the tech twenty dollars.

"Thank you so much," Anika said.

"Now let's get your eyebrows arched," Clifford said. The cosmetologist uses tweezers to pluck at Anika's eyebrows. It's a little painful. When Anika looks at the finished product, she doesn't like it at all. The cosmetologist plucked them way too thin.

"Now what do you want to do?" Clifford asked.

"It seems like the mall is closed so maybe we should head home," Anika said. Clifford was a little disappointed; he wanted to spend more time with Anika but she just didn't know Tampa that well and didn't know where else to go.

She receives a call from her photographer who was referred to her by a young actress she met at one of her presentations. This photographer had been an actor for fifteen years in California so he knows what the agents are looking for.

"I'm calling you to confirm the photo shoot for tomorrow. Let's talk about the wardrobe," the photographer said. Anika remembers that she has a hard time listening to professionals so she calls him back to get his input on fashions for acting. He told her to wear brown, black, or blue. Anika looked through her closet for the right clothes to wear. She finds a black shirt that would be perfect, but it got all twisted up in the washing machine and her mother had to fix it. The next day Anika drives to Tampa to meet the photographer. He was a young white man in his thirties. She handed him all six outfits and he picked out the best two. One outfit would be for her acting and the other would be a suit for press releases. Anika changed into her first outfit, the black shirt and blue jeans.

"Stand against the white wall. Now give me a smile. Perfect. Now put your chin down and move your hair out of your face. Yes, that looks good. You would be perfect for commercials because you have to have a big smile. Now laugh a little. Perfect. We're done with this shot. You can switch outfits," the photographer said. Anika switched to her black suit and wore the red shirt under the jacket.

"Just give me some smiles. This is for your press releases so we don't have to do any theatrical face shots. That blue fits well with your complexion. You have a beautiful complexion. And your makeup is flawless. We're done here. We all have the pictures we need. Give me about two weeks to send your pictures to you. You pick out the best two and I will photo shop them," the photographer said.

"I'm going to refer some people to you," Anika said.

"Thank you so much," the photographer said. Two weeks later she received her photos. She picked out her favorite two, emailed them to him and he touched them up. Anika is now ready for an agent. She has a resume, but it's very short. She did some acting in high school in the artistically talented program for actors, but after school, she just didn't have the passion to pursue acting. She doesn't have passion now for acting, but she's a natural at it so she figures this will aid her in her quest for fame. Her passion is being successful.

CHAPTER 22

Anika was at her favorite 24-hour store, shopping for some bras, when she ran into one of her uncles on her dad's side of the family. He was a tall man about 6 feet 2 inches. It had been ten years since she saw him last and she didn't recognize him. All that time had passed and Anika didn't get close to her family. Somehow she thought she wasn't related to them. "Anika," Thomas said. Anika turned to stare in his direction but did not recognize him. She held her nose to block the smell of alcohol from his breath.

"Anika, it's me, Uncle Thomas. Your daddy is my brother. I haven't seen your father in over twenty years. He just disappeared," Thomas said.

"I've seen him before. He was homeless and had serious mental problems. I don't think he was taking any medication," Anika said.

"I gave you my address at the funeral. How come you never wrote to me?" Thomas asked.

"I didn't think we were related," Anika said.

"Who gave you that idea?" Thomas asked.

"I don't know, maybe my state of mind at the time had something to do with it," Anika said.

"Well, you have a large family and a lot of them are here in Saint Pete. Follow me and I'll take you to your cousin's house." Anika followed Thomas as he parked his car in front of a mansion. There were five brand new cars in the driveway. The house was immaculate. It had several bathrooms and ten rooms, a living room, dining room, recreation room, and a home theatre.

The family just didn't go out to see movies anymore; they stayed indoors. They did all their shopping on the Internet. The only time they left the house was for church, birthday parties, holidays, weddings, and funerals. Anika's paternal grandmother died when her father was young, so his aunt raised him. And then his Aunt Shelly died and left her daughter, Teresa, her large savings account. Shelly had invested her money in the stock market and came out on top. She didn't spend it when she was alive, living modestly. Teresa had three children, Derrick, Lindsey, and Stephanie, which made them Anika's second cousins. And the three of them had children, which made them Anika's third cousins. Thomas explained all of this to Anika before they rang the doorbell and Teresa answered it providing a warm smile and enough room to allow for entry. She was a short woman with impaired vision. Anika thought about having an anxiety attack, but it didn't happen. The attacks seem to happen when she was doing something stressful. There's a rectangle swimming pool in the living room with plants propped up against it. Anika could not believe her eyes. She never knew her family was rich. She was used to struggling on her disability check.

"Who do we have here?" Teresa asked.

"This is your long lost cousin. Her father is Masjid who is your cousin," Thomas said.

"Yes, I'm sorry I didn't keep in contact with you. I was having mental health issues and wasn't aware that you were my family. Anxiety has been playing a large role in my life lately and I'm trying to work through it with a psychotherapist," Anika said.

"Are you taking medication for your anxiety attacks?" Teresa asked.

"Yes," Anika said.

"And you're still getting the anxiety attacks?" Teresa asked.

"Yes, I am," Anika replied.

"I used to get anxiety attacks. You have to figure out a way to get rid of them. Tell yourself that you're doing well whenever you think about the anxiety attack," Teresa said.

"Ok, I'll try that," Anika said.

"Let me introduce you to my children. This is Derrick, Lindsey, and Stephanie. Stephanie has a BA in Psychology also. You too will probably get along," Teresa said.

All three of her children are adults now and they introduce Anika to their kids. Anika has seven fourth cousins.

"So what have you been doing with your life, Anika?" Stephanie asked.

"I'm an author now. I made the paper several times," Anika said.

"We're going to have someone famous in the family," Derrick said.

Anika begins to chuckle.

"Yes, you will," Anika said. Anika grabs some of the newspaper articles out of the car and passes them out to all the family.

"Some more of the family might come over here tomorrow. I'll let you know," Teresa said. Anika went on to work. She was afraid of having another anxiety attack. She began to take the incoming calls. When there was a break in between calls, Anika begins to talk to herself.

"You're doing well. You're not going to have an anxiety attack." Anika couldn't believe it was working.

"Maybe this will work every time," Anika thought. Her supervisor then took a seat next to her. She thanked God, she didn't experience an anxiety attack in front of her supervisor. "I'm going to monitor you today, Anika. Your scores are good. Don't be nervous; I'm here to give you feedback," Her supervisor said. Anika took a few calls and her supervisor listened.

"Do you know what went wrong on that last call?" The supervisor asked.

"No, I don't," Anika said.

"You didn't acknowledge the respondent's concern. You first must acknowledge the concern and then provide a persuader. Maybe you would have gotten the respondent to agree to do the survey. Do you understand?" The supervisor asked.

"Yes, I do," Anika said.

"You're doing an excellent job," the supervisor said. The rest of the night, Anika went through the calls without an anxiety attack. She felt that she was the one in control of avoiding the anxiety attacks, but she will still take her medicine because it helps her sleep.

CHAP T E R 2 3

Anika meets with her psychotherapist again.

"How is the medicine working? Are you having any more anxiety attacks?" Sanders asked.

"The medicine helps me sleep but I don't think it's getting rid of my anxiety attacks. I figure I have to find a way to do that on my own. I told myself that I was doing well when I started thinking about the anxiety attacks at work and the anxiety attack didn't happen. Can you write me a three-month prescription? I can't afford to keep coming every month," Anika said.

"Yes, I will," Sanders said.

Anika went home and checked her mail. Her two photos arrived. She can now start looking for an agent. She contacts the first agent on her list and they want her to submit her resume and head shot so she does just that. Two weeks later they agree to bring her aboard. They began by sending her out on auditions. She gets one audition per week, trying to get a part in any production. After a month passes, Anika landed a role in a low budget movie. She felt she had to start somewhere and wondered how she would handle it if she got an anxiety attack while filming. The camera picks up everything and would pick up her slurred speech and trembling mouth. She never suffers from anxiety while doing something fun so she wasn't too worried. She rushed over to Clifford's house to give him the good news. Besides her mom, he's about the only one she can trust with her dreams. When she arrived at his house, she sees his door wide open.

"Hey baby you're not afraid of someone coming into your home and harming you?" Anika said.

"No that's what guns are for," Clifford said.

"I did a study on guns in the home and I learned that a large percent of people end up hurting themselves with the gun instead of protecting themselves," Anika said.

"I'm from the country where everybody has a gun so those statistics aren't true."

"If I asked you to get rid of it, would you?" Anika asked.

"Please don't ask me to get rid of my gun. I have to protect my family," Clifford said.

"Promise me you'll never show me where it's at," Anika said.

"Why?" Clifford asked.

"Because of my mental illness, I'm afraid I may accidentally use it on myself," Anika said.

"What would you say if I put a two carat diamond on your finger?" Clifford asked. Anika begins to laugh.

"I can't think of marriage right now because the government will take part of my disability check away," Anika said.

"How much do you get from disability?" Clifford asked.

"Nine hundred and thirty five dollars a month," Anika said.

"I can afford that," Clifford said.

"I want you to go to the Masjid with me. It starts at 1pm," Anika said.

"Ok, let's go," Clifford said.

They pull up to the Masjid and see Umar speaking to a group of men.

"Friday is a good day for prayer. I've always said that. There's a new program at Eckerd College that's helping business owners grow their business and for all others who want to attend, please load up in the van."

"I've been trying for years to get my book out there, but I got little help from the community. This will be a good opportunity for me," Anika said. Anika and Clifford followed the van to the College. There were five business owners that loaded up in the van.

When they got to the college an older man who looked to be in his early seventies greeted everyone at the door. Thomas whispered in Umar's ear.

"I thought I said a few people," Thomas said and they both begin to chuckle.

"Let me introduce myself. My name is Thomas and it's my passion to help business owners make it to the top. We're starting a new program here at Eckerd College that will take business owners to the next level. We have students that are ready to help you. We have lawyers and people that can help you market your business and we even provide financial assistance, if you qualify." Anika was so excited to hear this, she immediately stood and introduced herself.

"Hello, my name is Anika Muhammad and I'm an author. I've been struggling on my own for four years now, with no help. I've gotten in the Florida Sentinel, and St. Pete Bulletin, and N Touch News. I've spoken for the Saint Petersburg Islamic Center, SPC College, and the Pinellas County Urban League.

I'm selling five books at a time when I'm out and about, but for four years now, I haven't had any online orders. I have a blog and I get sixty thousand hits per month and I have three hundred thousand comments to approve. It was taking me eight hours a day to approve them and I wasn't selling anything so I just stopped. I want to end the stigma of mental health and I know this will be big. I just need a little help from an organization like yours," Anika said.

Clifford rubs her back in approval.

"You have a lot of passion. We are going to create an application that you can fill out and then we will let you know if we can approve it," the gentleman said.

"This may be your chance to make it Anika," Clifford said.

CHAPTER 24

Anika left Clifford and walked into her mother's house and couldn't believe who she saw. Mosi. Mosi stands to his feet. He had lost fifty pounds. You could see the bones in his face. The five years apart from Anika didn't do him any good. "Anika," Mosi said as he walked closer to her. Anika could not believe her eyes. She was speechless. She had finally found the one and now Mosi steps into her life. Mosi gives her a hug.

"I received your letter, but I didn't know how to respond. Anika I have Aids," Mosi said.

"I'm gay," Mosi said.

"I know Mosi. I could never accept the fact that you were gay. It was too much for me to take at the time. When I got sick years ago and some spirit warned me about Aids, I didn't understand the message at the time. It was an unseen man's voice coming from the TV set. He said, "I know it's hard for you to concentrate now, but I need you to listen, Aids, vitamin c, flowers, abuse." Years later I figured out the message. I figured out that you would get Aids. You're going to be ok Mosi. I want you to take a look at my book. I'm a published author," Anika said. Mosi takes the book in his hands, looks at the front, turns a few pages and looks at the back.

"How much is the book?" Mosi asked.
"Twenty dollars," Anika said.

"Twenty dollars for this?" Mosi said with a calm look on his face. Anika was crushed. She put her heart and soul into that book and that's all he can thing to say? Mosi runs to the toilet and throws up. Anika kneels on the cold floor and rubs his back.

163

"It was a long time since I wrote you Mosi. A lot has happened since then. I have a boyfriend. He wants to marry me Mosi," Anika said.

"You're beautiful. I can expect another man to be interested in you. But I had to come to say I'm sorry for cheating on you," Mosi said.

"I've always wanted to know. When did you become gay?" Anika said.

"You were the first woman I ever had sex with, but I started sleeping with men when I turned sixteen," Mosi said.

"You're not gay Mosi. I know myself, how much you love sex with a woman. Are you sleeping with men now?" Anika asked.

"No, I'm afraid to spread the disease. Anika I don't want to fight this battle by myself. I need you. What if I don't make it?" Mosi said.

"Are you taking any medication?" Anika asked.
"I'm taking medicine now and it's making me sick to my stomach. I think I'm going to stop taking it," Mosi said.

"You came here for a reason Mosi, so I can save your life. Don't stop taking your medication. You can live a long time as long as you listen to your doctor. Look how hard it was for me to take medication," Anika said.

"So did you ever figure out if the drugs were making you sick or was it a mental illness?" Mosi asked.

"I can accept it now. I have schizophrenia. You know how I can stay up for two days and film TV shows and not get tired," Anika said.

"What ever happened to your TV shows? Why did you stop?" Mosi asked.

"Never let anyone kill your dreams Mosi. Keep your dreams to yourself. I told the wrong person and she told me I would never make it as a TV producer, so I lost my passion," Anika said.

"You have to get your passion back. You're the one who tells everyone to never give up," Mosi said. The front door opens all of a sudden. Clifford uses the key given to him by Ms. Muhammad, who thinks of him as a son. He walks in and into the bathroom. Clifford looks down at Anika as she holds Mosi in her arms.

"What the fuck is going on Anika?!" Clifford said. Anika snatches her arms away from Mosi.

"Clifford this is Mosi," Anika said.

"I know who the fuck this is? I've seen the pictures. What the fuck are you doing here?" Clifford said.

"Clifford let me explain. I wrote him a letter a while back before I met you. I wanted him back," Anika said.

"How can you want him back, he's gay?" Clifford said. Mosi struggles to pick his own self up from the toilet seat.

"How could you tell him that Anika? That was between you and me. I confided in you," Mosi said.

"So now, what? You want him now?" Clifford said. Anika remains silent. She never fell out of love with Mosi. She cares for Clifford but she is not in love with him. She and Mosi used to talk for hours, and Clifford barely calls her. What is she going to do? Ms. Muhammad walks into the house and is in shock to see Mosi.

Mosi I can't believe it's you. You're so skinny. Are you sick?" Ms. Muhammad asked.

"Mama, Mosi has Aids," Anika said.

"Aids?! Do you have Aids Anika?" Clifford asked.

"Baby, I promise I'll get checked," Anika said.

"Oh, I can't take this shit. You mean to tell me you could have given me Aids? What the fuck is going on?" Clifford said.

"Hey, watch who you're talking to. I'm still in love with this woman," Mosi said. Mosi almost faints and Anika catches him.

"Oh hell no!" Clifford said.

"Mosi you have to leave. I can't be with you. I'm with Clifford now," Anika said.

"But do you love him?" Mosi asked. Anika is silent.

"Do you still love me Anika?" Mosi asked.

"Yes, I do, but I can't be with you. Once I get into a committed relationship I stay that way. Mosi you have to leave." A tear falls from Mosi's eye. Ms. Muhammad holds Mosi up.

"Let me walk you to your car Mosi," Ms. Muhammad said. Mosi keeps an eye on Anika as he walks out.

"So what are you going to do?" Clifford asked.

"I'm going to stay with you Clifford. We can go get tested together, but we used protection so if I do have anything you wouldn't have caught anything." The next day Anika and Clifford drive over to the clinic to get tested. They both are HIV negative. Mosi caught Aids after he broke up with Anika. Anika wondered if she would ever see Mosi again. She can't reach out to him now because she's in a committed relationship with Clifford. And this is the best relationship she's ever had.

Anika prepares her business plan with excitement. She figures she needs ten thousand dollars to start her business. She rushes over to Clifford's house to show him what she has developed.

"I want to bring Hollywood to St. Petersburg," Anika said.

"You can't do that. You have to relocate in order to make it," Clifford said.

"I don't agree. All I need is the money," Anika said.

"Well, if you keep doing things for free you'll never be able to afford Hollywood. Look at your business plan. You're only charging one-hundred dollars per speech. It's going to take more than that to get a lawyer to look over your contract," Clifford said.

"How much do you think I should charge?" Anika asked.

"The standard rate for a speaker to start off with is three-thousand dollars. That's how much you should charge. And you should ask for half up front to book the date," Clifford said.

"Yes, you're right. I did read in one of my books that most speakers start off charging twenty-five hundred dollars," Anika said.

"If you knew that, why would you short change your-self?" Clifford asked.

"I was just taking advice from my friends," Anika said.

"Stick with me and I'll make you rich," Clifford said.

No one ever believed in Anika before. Not even Mosi. Anika feels blessed to finally find someone that cares about her dreams. She has to wait a month to present her business plan to Eckerd College. She is so worried about what they may say. She needs six thousand dollars to pay for a publicist, one thousand for a computer, one thousand for some suits, and one thousand to buy some books and she doesn't have good credit. She started off having good credit in college but decided to get some credit cards which was a bad mistake. She lost her job and couldn't afford the payments. She would ask Mosi for money, but he would always refuse. If only she would have held on to her financial aid money instead of blowing it on clothes and junk food she would have had enough to pay her bills on time. She'd learn from her mistakes.

CHAPTER 25

Two months have gone by and Anika has not heard from Mosi. She thinks it's for the best. Anika walks into Clifford's house and the lights are off. He has lilac candles burning throughout the house. A trail of rose petals leads to his bedroom. Upon entering she sees Clifford is lying on the bed wearing a silk robe. "This is for you baby," Clifford said.

"What are we celebrating?" Anika asked.

"My love for you," Clifford said. Clifford undresses Anika. He kisses her softly on her shoulders.

"I love you Anika. I want you to be my wife," Clifford said.

"One day that will happen," Anika said.

"Yes it will," Clifford said. Clifford lifts Anika in his arms and places her naked body on the bed. He makes love to her.

"Let's go out for dinner. There's this new restaurant on Gandy that I've been wanting to go to for a long time," Anika said.

"You know I'll take you anywhere. You just ask me," Clifford said.

"You are the one for me. I knew it when I first met you. I don't want anyone else," Anika said.

"Neither do I," Clifford said. Anika's phone begins to ring. It's Rachel.

"Anika you will not believe who I just saw," Rachel said.

"Who?" Anika questioned.

"I saw Mosi. He introduced me to his girlfriend. He said he wanted to thank you for telling him to take his medicine. You saved his life Anika," Rachel said.

"Well, I'm glad to hear that," Anika said.

"So do you still have feelings for him?" Rachel instigated.

"I will always love Mosi but I can't be with him so I'm glad he moved on and he is healthy. That makes me feel real good," Anika said.

"I thought he was gay," Rachel said.

"No, I don't think he's gay at all. I do believe some people get molested or raped and they become confused with their identity. That's probably what happened to Mosi. He loves women. You know how much he loved me and for many years. I told him I thought he wasn't gay and he listened to me. So I'm happy now," Anika said.

"So you're not going to try to get back with him?" Rachel said.

"I saw Mosi. He introduced me to his girlfriend. He said he wanted to thank you for telling him to take his medicine. You saved his life Anika," Rachel said.

"Well, I'm glad to hear that," Anika said.

"So do you still have feelings for him?" Rachel instigated.

"I will always love Mosi but I can't be with him so I'm glad he moved on and he is healthy. That makes me feel real good," Anika said.

"I thought he was gay," Rachel said.

"No, I don't think he's gay at all. I do believe some people get molested or raped and they become confused with their identity.

That's probably what happened to Mosi. He loves women. You know how much he loved me and for many years. I told him I thought he wasn't gay and he listened to me. So I'm happy now," Anika said.

"So you're not going to try to get back with him?" Rachel said.

"No Rachel I have someone," Anika said.

"Who, who do you have?" Rachel said.

"Rachel, do you have anyone? I never remember you having someone. All I remember is you trying to get into my business," Anika said.

"Well, that's rude. I wasn't trying to get into your business. I was just curious, that's all. I'll leave you alone then," Rachel said and then hangs up the phone.

"So that was nosey Rachel?" Clifford said.

"Yes," Anika said.

"So I'm glad that Mosi moved on. Now I don't have to worry about him messing up our relationship," Clifford said.

"I'm over Mosi. When I met you, you were all that I could think about," Anika said. Clifford took Anika to dinner and he laughed at how fast she began to eat, like she was starving. The next day Anika prepares to act in her first movie. She had been studying the script for a few months and now it was time to put her acting skills to the test. She starred in a low budget gangster movie called Bust, It was shot by the most popular movie director in Saint Petersburg. Anika finally got her chance to show off her true talent.

The director would shoot for two hours a day and pay her one-hundred dollars. Clifford thought she should be charging more, but that's between her agent and director. The other actors had to take hundreds of takes to get it right. Anika was a natural and it only took her a few takes.

CHAP T E R 2 6

Anika scheduled a meeting with a center that offers free counseling to businesses. She wanted to go over her business plan
for Eckerd College. She needed ten thousand dollars and hoped
that Eckerd College would be able to loan her the money. She
messed up her credit in college by using credit cards and not
paying off the balances because she couldn't find work. Mosi
wouldn't help her pay any of her bills even though he was an
electrical engineer with plenty of money and good credit. Anika
handed her business plan to Mr. Warren for him to look over. Anika's mission statement was that her business is one that offers
presentations and books to the community to end the stigma of
mental illness, and encourage medication therapy.
She plans to charge twenty-five hundred dollars to tell her story
to organizations, churches, library's, book stores, and confer-
ences. She also planned to sell her book.
Mr. Warren looks over her business plan and then places the
paper on the table.

"You have too much going on in your mission statement. You're not going to end the stigma of mental illness and
you shouldn't mention encouraging medication therapy. It's too
much," Warren said.

"I want to provide mental health motivational speeches
to the community," Anika said.

"Then that's what you should say." 'Angels is a company that provides mental health motivational speaking to the community.' It says here you're charging twenty-five hundred dollars to do speeches. That's too much," Warren said.

Warren draws a pyramid and puts speakers making fifty thousand dollars or more at the top and he put a line down at the bottom to indicate that Anika is below all of the speakers.

"You see, this is where you are right now; you're at the bottom. You should charge two-hundred-fifty dollars to do a speech. I don't even make twenty- five hundred dollars yet and I've done a lot of speeches," Warren said.

"But I have to hire a lawyer to look over my contract. Wouldn't that cost a lot?" Anika asked.

"You only have to pay the lawyer once. Now let me look at your website. I see you have, "Welcome," at the top of the home page. It doesn't even say what you do. I think most people will click right off the website. You should put, "The best mental health motivational speaker." And I see you have a media kit page. Where is your bio? You should have a bio up here. Take away the newspaper articles. And I want to see a press kit that you write about yourself," Warren said.

"I've always felt like I was normal and I thought normal people don't get mental illnesses," Anika said.

"That's good. Write as your topic, 'You are normal, too.'" Warren said.

"I also want to know who my target market is. Is there a company I can pay to find this out?" Anika questioned.

"Why pay someone when we can do it for free. I wouldn't put an age or gender on your target market. Your target market is anyone who wants to help others and people with mental illness. We can schedule another meeting. We can meet as much as you'd like," Warren said.

"Ok, thank you," Anika said.

Anika heads over to Clifford's house.

"So how was the meeting with the business coach?" Clifford asked.

"I think he was a little negative. He said I shouldn't charge twenty-five hundred dollars for a speech. He said that he doesn't even get paid that much. He said that I am at the bottom," Anika said.

"I think you should charge at least five hundred dollars. I don't think you're way at the bottom. I'm sure there are people who have never been in the newspapers or on the radio who are charging five hundred dollars for their speeches. You are starting to build a fan base so you should ask for five-hundred and not a penny less. You have high self-esteem, but low self-worth. You are worth five thousand dollars a speech if you can save somebody's life. Just one life is worth that much. Maybe Eckerd College can help you grow a fan base," Clifford said.

"Yes, I'm hoping," Anika said.

CHAPTER 27

Anika sits on the couch in her mother's house and it looks like she has a protruding stomach. "Anika come here," Ms. Muhammad said. She pokes at Anika's stomach.

"Your stomach is getting big. Do you think it's filling up with fluid again like it did five years ago when your lungs collapsed?" Ms. Muhammad asked.

"I don't know. I hope I'm not pregnant," Anika said.

"You should go to the hospital," Ms. Muhammad said.

"I'll wait for two months until the cycle ends at my job and I'm not working," Anika said.

"No, you should go now before the fluid builds up again and you start coughing and your lungs end up collapsing again," Ms. Muhammad said.

"I'm doing so well now. That would really stop my progress. I was mad at God when my lungs collapsed. I didn't learn anything from that painful experience and it didn't cause me to become close to God. I'm not going to be mad at God this time. I understand that our bodies go through trials and tribulations naturally," Anika said.

"You did learn something. I think your lungs collapsed because you had massive amounts of cocaine in your system. You were trusting Mary to have your back when she didn't and you were sick from not taking your medication and you were leaving your water bottles everywhere. Anybody could have slipped you cocaine.

If you would have accepted that you had a mental disorder and taken the medicine you would have never been hospitalized and you wouldn't have been so careless with a lack of concern for your well-being. Remember I said that life is 1% what happens to you and 99% how you react to it. Before you were hospitalized you saw faces in the sheets, rugs, and walls and you were depressed all the time. Because of your studies, you knew this was a warning sign of mental illness, but you would not admit that you had a problem and refused medication," Ms. Muhammad said.

"Yes, you're right. I'm going to drive myself to the hospital."

Anika heads over to the hospital. The receptionist asked her to fill out a form to be admitted. The receptionist places arm bands with her name and age around Anika's wrist. Anika goes to sit down. There are about twenty people waiting to be seen, including an African American couple.

"How long have you been waiting?" Anika asked.

"Too long," Patricia said. After five minutes the medical assistant calls Anika.

"How can I help you today?" The medical assistant asked.

"My stomach is getting big. I think my lungs are filling up with fluid again," Anika said.

"Have you ever had surgery?" The medical assistant asked.

'Yes, twice. They scrapped my lungs because they collapsed," Anika said.

"Ok, have a seat in the waiting area and we will give you a call," the medical assistant said. Anika only had to wait five minutes. Her condition was serious. The doctors always see the life threatening cases first. Her nurse walked her over to the emergency rooms.

"Hello, I'm your nurse, Janet. What seems to be the problem?" Janet asked.

"My stomach is getting big. I think fluid might be building up in my lungs," Anika said. Janet places an IV in Anika's arm.

"Is there a possibility that you may be pregnant?" Janet asked.

"Yes," Anika said.

"Please go by the nurse's station and give me a sample of your urine. I'm going to test you to see if you're pregnant," Janet said. Anika takes a cup from the bathroom counter and fills it with urine and hands it over to the nurse. Anika waits for ten minutes for the results. She felt a little nervous.

"What if I am pregnant? I won't have an abortion, but maybe I can give my child up for adoption. I don't have the money to raise a child and a child would interfere with my career," Anika thought. The nurse came back into the room. Anika's heart began to pound.

"You're not pregnant. I'm going to send you to get a chest x-ray," Janet said. The orderly wheels Anika into the x-ray room. She undresses and puts on her gown. Anika stands in front of the x-ray machine.

"Lift your arms all the way up and hold the bar. I'm going to tell you when to hold your breath," the technician said. Anika struggles to put her arms up. The IV is causing her pain.

"It's hard for me to put my arms all the way up because of this IV," Anika said.

"Maybe it wasn't put in right; it shouldn't hurt. Ok, hold your breath. Now breathe out. Stand with your shoulders against the x-ray machine. Now hold your breath. Now breathe out. Ok, we're done. It will take a few minutes for your doctor to look at the results," the technician said. The orderly wheels Anika back into the emergency room. Anika waits for ten minutes for her doctor to come in. She calls up her boyfriend.

"I'm in the hospital baby," Anika said.

"Oh no why?" Clifford said.

"I may have fluid in my lung again. My right lung collapsed five years ago and they had to do surgery," Anika said.

"It's good that you went right to the emergency room. We have a lot in common. The same thing happened to me. They had to take away part of my lung, but I'm still able to breathe," Clifford said.

"I didn't know that. My doctor just walked in, I'll call you later," Anika said.

"Ok, keep me updated," Clifford said.

"Hello I'm your doctor. You do have fluid in your lungs, but it's not enough to remove it. I'm going to order a CT scan to see if this is new fluid or old fluid," the doctor said. Anika is wheeled over to another room for a full body CT scan where the technologist greets Anika.

"Hello, I'm Phil and I'm going to be administering your CT scan. When I put the fluid in your IV, it will make you feel like you have to urinate. The machine will tell you when to hold your breath". The technologist starts up the CT scan. Anika lies down on the machine. The machine moves her through an oval opening. The machine speaks.

"Hold your breath. Breathe out. Hold your breath again. Now breathe out. You're all done. The doctor will give you your results."

Anika calls Clifford.

"They found fluid in my lungs and gave me a CT scan. My lungs are ok and I'm not pregnant, so why is my stomach swelling up?" Anika questioned.

"Who said you were pregnant?" Clifford asked.

"My family was wondering why my stomach was getting big. I thought I might be pregnant," Anika said.

"Well, I know you're not pregnant," Clifford said.

"My doctors coming in. I'm going to put you on speaker phone so you can hear what she says," Anika said.

"We checked the fluid in your lungs and it was old fluid. It was nothing new. And your lungs are fine," the doctor said.

"Then why is my stomach swollen?" Anika asked.

"I suggest you buy some Colace, a stool softener and follow up with Johnnie Ruth Clarke clinic within 72 hours. Return to the ER for chest pain, shortness of breath, or any concerns," the doctor said and then left Anika to dress herself.

"You're going to have a huge doctor bill," Clifford said.

"Yes, I know and I don't have the money to pay it. Thank God Medicare will cover most of the cost. I'm going to come see you," Anika said. Anika gets into her car to drive over to her boyfriend's house. She started thinking again, '*what if I get another anxiety attack because I'm driving to Tampa? I need to call someone.*' Anika calls Clifford, again.

"I had to call you. I need someone to talk to so I won't get another anxiety attack," Anika said.

"I thought you stopped getting those," Clifford said.

"I thought so too. I believe my mind is so powerful that I'm creating these anxiety attacks. They started one day when I didn't have my medicine. I said to myself, what if I lose my mind because I don't have my medicine? And then I started feeling like I would lose my mind. But it's not the same feeling I feel when I am about to really lose my mind and be hospitalized. Whenever that used to happen, I would have racing thoughts. My mind can't concentrate on one thing because I'm busy thinking about what I need to be doing, and where I need to be, and what might happen to me. But the time my friends were smoking marijuana around me, I didn't have any racing thoughts. I just started to hallucinate and a few days later I was in the hospital. At that time there were warning signs that I was mentally becoming sick. I started seeing faces in the sheets again and I heard music in my head," Anika said.

"Boy you have been through a lot," Clifford said.

"Yes, I have," Anika said. Anika made it to Clifford's house without an anxiety attack, but on her way back to St. Petersburg she got that feeling of having a possible onset of anxiety.

She thought about calling her cousin, but realized her cousin was probably at work. She didn't even think about calling her boyfriend again. She was almost home when the anxiety attack started. She began to drive forty-five miles per hour on the highway fearing that she'd get into a car accident. Drivers speed by her irate. Her mouth started moving uncontrollably.

"There must be a way to get rid of these attacks. There has to be something I can tell myself to make them stop," Anika thought. She made it home safe and thanked God. As soon as she enters her mother's home she grabs for her anxiety medication. She lies down and falls asleep in fifteen minutes. Before the medication she used to stay up for two days with the anxiety attack, two whole days suffering nonstop. She has to see her doctor again.

"Maybe I do need counseling," Anika thought.

CHAPTER 28

Anika drives over to her psychotherapist office. She's always on time and used to having to wait thirty minutes to see a nurse practitioner at the other mental health facility she used to go to. It was swamped with patients. Most of them couldn't afford the care they were getting but since the facility was non-profit the staff didn't pressure the patients for payment.

"So you want to talk?" Dr. Sanders asked.

"Yes, I'm still getting anxiety attacks. The medicine works to put me to sleep, but it doesn't stop my anxiety attacks. I was molested by my brother when I was young and I never got counseling for it," Anika said.

"Do you feel guilty?" Dr. Sanders asked.

"No. I know now that it wasn't my fault that it happened. A little girl molested my brother when he was eight and then he molested me. He didn't know what he was doing.

"Tell me what do you experience when you have an anxiety attack?" Dr. Sanders asked.

"I feel like I'm going to lose my mind again. I get slurred speech and I constantly move my mouth uncontrollably," Anika said.

"What happened when you lost your mind?" Dr. Sanders asked.

"I was dancing, I thought I was Hitler, I saw a vision of Jesus, I thought I saw God, a man's voice from the TV warned me about Mosi getting Aids," Anika said.

"So are you afraid you will experience a relapse again?" Dr. Sanders asked.

"Yes. I'm afraid to be embarrassed. I never have anxiety attacks while giving speeches or while acting. It usually happens when I'm driving to Tampa or when I'm working," Anika said.

"Are you under severe stress?" Dr. Sanders asked. "No, but driving is stressful. My job is not stressful at all and I still get anxiety attacks," Anika said.

"Do you know when it's about to happen?" Dr. Sanders asked.

"Yes. I'll first start thinking that I may get an anxiety attack and then it happens," Anika said.

"What you are experiencing is anticipatory anxiety. Tell yourself that your last relapse was five years ago and it's not going to happen again," Dr. Sanders said.

"One of my friends on Facebook told me to write down on one side of the paper everything I'm afraid of happening and then on the other side of the paper write down what I'm going to do to stop the anxiety attacks. I'm going to try this and see if it works," Anika said.

"Yes, that could work. Try that," Dr. Sanders said.

"I think that I do have paranoid schizophrenia. I think you're miss diagnosing me," Anika said.

"And why do you say that?" Dr. Sanders asked.

"When I was young I didn't care to make friends, I have slurred speech, my grandmother has schizophrenia, I have short term memory loss and when I was sick, I saw faces everywhere, and I was always paranoid that my boyfriend was cheating on me.

I used to harass him. I've told you very little and I don't understand how you could give a diagnosis in such short amount of time," Anika said. The doctor didn't say a word she just wrote in her notepad.

"When do you feel you need to see me the next time?" Dr. Sanders asked.

"At least every month for counseling," Anika said.

"Ok, I will schedule you in for next month," Dr. Sanders said. Anika drives home and lies on her bed. She notices a letter placed on her bed from social security. Her heart began to beat. She always gets nervous when she gets a letter from them because she's paranoid they may take her disability away. She reads the letter out loud.

"We have received your file from the social security administration to determine whether you meet the requirement for disability benefits. After reviewing your case, we find we need more information about your condition. Therefore, we have arranged the following appointment for you, which we will pay for from funds provided by social security. You must meet with Carol Rinehart , Monday, February 1 at 4pm." Anika looked down at her watch and realized it was 3:30 pm. She begins to panic. She starts thinking about getting an anxiety attack so she searches through her purse for instructions on just what to do when this type of thing occurs. The anxiety attacks always go away when she does speeches so she starts to say her speech in her head to avoid an onset. It worked! She rushes to her car to drive over to see this disability doctor and arrives ten minutes early and wipes the sweat from her forehead.

"Hello, I'm Carol. You may have a seat. The Social Security Disability office told me you were coming. Tell me about your illness," Dr. Rinehart said.

Anika knew the doctor diagnosed her with schizoaffective bipolar type. She knew this was a lesser disorder and they may take away her disability because of it. She has to somehow convince the doctor that she has paranoid schizophrenia. The initial diagnosis that social security based her disability determination upon was paranoid schizophrenia.

"I'm paranoid schizophrenic. I was paranoid that my boyfriend was cheating on me when he wasn't. I hallucinated. I thought I saw God and I dreamed of seeing Jesus and I thought I was the reincarnation of Hitler," Anika said.

"When was the last time you hallucinated?" Dr. Rinehart asked.

"It was five years ago. I was hospitalized six times because I refused to take my medication. I thought I was normal and normal people don't get mental illness," Anika said.

"What medications are you taking now?" Dr. Rinehart asked. Anika looked for her medications in her purse.

"I'm taking clonazepam, clomipramine, and Geodon," Anika said.

"What is for the paranoid schizophrenia?" Dr. Rinehart asked.

"The Geodon is for the paranoid schizophrenia, and the clomipramine is for my OCD, and the clonazepam is for my anxiety attacks," Anika said.
"What do you do when you're experiencing obsessive compulsive disorder?" Dr. Rinehart asked.

"When I'm really sick I put things together in threes and I always have to look up and to my right," Anika said. Do you hear voices?" Dr. Rinehart asked.

"I used to hear a man in my television set," Anika said.

"I want you to add five to nineteen. What do you get?" Dr. Rinehart asked.

"Twenty four," Anika said.

"Spell the word, 'world' backwards," Dr. Rinehart said.

"Dlorw," Anika said.

"I'm going to name three things. I want to see if you can remember them, chair, picture, wall."

"Chair, picture, wall," Anika said.

"Good. I think you do have paranoid schizophrenia and you have all your paperwork so you have nothing to worry about. We will continue your disability," Dr. Rinehart said. Anika was able to breathe again. She exhaled. She immediately called up her boyfriend.

"I thought they were going to take away my disability. I got this letter that I needed to see a doctor. I was so scared," Anika said.

"You shouldn't worry. All that you been through they can't possibly take away your disability. I think you don't have any faith. You have a one way connection to God and Jesus and you don't know how to use your gift," Clifford said.

"What do you mean?" Anika questioned.

"All you have to do is pray for your book to become a best seller and your book will start flying off the shelves. You need to read the bible so you can know who God is," Clifford said.

"I think the bible is a road map directing you to do the right thing. The bible has been rewritten. A lot of what God actually revealed has been lost.

If God speaks to me in my dreams when I do something wrong, why do I need to read the bible?" Anika asked.

"Because you need to know who God is," Clifford said.

"I think I know God more than most people. I saw him for God sakes," Anika said.

"If you were using your gifts you would be famous by now," Clifford said.

"All I need is a publicist. I have everything else," Anika said.

"God can do more for you than any ole' publicist. All you have to do is ask him for his help," Clifford said.

"Ok, tonight I will pray for him to help me by the end of February," Anika said.

CHAP T E R 2 9

Anika waits patiently for Clifford to finish studying the bible. He is nondenominational. He studies his bible on Friday from 6pm to Saturday 7pm. He keeps his phone on silent, ignoring the calls. Anika does not like this at all. It reminds her of when she experienced depression. She didn't pick up phone calls from family and friends. At 7:30pm the phone rings. It is Clifford. "Baby I got some good ideas. I'm going to bring Hollywood to Saint Petersburg," Anika said.

"Why don't you try selling your books to white people? Black people are not buying your books. You keep putting ads in the paper and you only sell one book," Clifford said.

"I sell books all the time. How can you study the Bible for fifteen hours and come out so negative? The purpose of putting advertisements in the newspapers is, so they would write articles about me so I can build a press kit; it's not only for selling books. When I get connected to a speaking bureau then I can travel all over the United States and do lectures and sell books," Anika said.

"You're talking about bringing Hollywood to St. Petersburg and making billions. You have to have a reason for Hollywood to come to St. Petersburg," Clifford said.

"You were telling me that I don't have faith in God. I have faith to move mountains. You're the one that doesn't have faith," Anika said.

"No, I don't have any faith in your book," Clifford said. Anika gasps for air.

"I like the book, but it's not a million dollar seller," Clifford said.

"A book doesn't have to be good to become a best seller. It just has to have major marketing. You don't know shit about marketing and you don't know shit about publishing. You didn't even know what a press kit was," Anika said.

"The area of St. Pete isn't feelin' you. You're not selling any books. You have to leave St. Pete in order to make it," Clifford said.

"I'm going to make you eat your words!" Anika screams in frustration and disappointment.

"If that's how you're going to talk to me, I'm getting off the phone," Clifford said. A week went by and the two of them barely even said a word to each other. Saturday rolled around before Anika finally decided to text Clifford. She knew he was studying the bible and probably wouldn't respond.

"I need to talk to you," Anika texted.

"What about baby?" Clifford asked. Anika didn't respond. She waited for him to call her.

"What is it you wanted to talk about?" Clifford asked.

"If we're going to stay in this relationship you have to watch what you say to me," Anika said.

"You messed up my Sabbath to rehash this old mess. The reason why I told you nobody's feeling you is because you keep spending your money on this book and you're not getting any results. You're wasting your money," Clifford said.

"I don't want to talk about my career anymore. I'm going to keep that part of my life to myself," Anika said.

"I will still help you," Clifford said.

"I don't want any of your help. I'm going to get a full time job and pay for a publicist myself," Anika said.

"You keep putting these ads in the newspaper and for what?" Clifford said.

"So I can get a press kit," Anika said.

"So what have you done with your press kit?" Clifford asked.

"None of your business," Anika said.

"You see, you're telling me I need to watch what I say and you say things like that," Clifford said.

"That's not mean. I just told you I don't want to talk about my career. Why are you asking me about my press kit? So you can give me negative feedback?"

"So did you get everything off your chest? Because I'm going to get back to my studying," Clifford said.

"Yes, bye," Anika said.

Seven days went by and Anika did not receive a phone call from Clifford but she did receive a call from Attiq.

"How have you been?" Attiq asked.

"I'm doing fine," Anika said. "You know I miss you. I want to see you," Attiq said.

"No. You wouldn't take me out and you wanted me to change the way I dress because it's not Muslim-like. You continually pressured me to have sex and you know Muslim women are not supposed to have sex before marriage, according to the Quran. "

191

"I didn't realize I was doing wrong. I'm a changed man. Do you want to go out to dinner?" Attiq asked.

"I'll think about it. I'm in a relationship," Anika said.

"Tell me about this man. How old is he?" Attiq asked.

"I don't want to talk about him," Anika said.

"Well, you talked about me. People telling me that you told them I took you to my house and tried to have sex with you," Attiq said.

"When you do the wrong thing, people will talk. I've learned not to share information about old boyfriends with new boyfriends. I'm no longer discussing my relationship problems with my friends," Anika said.

"That's what I was telling you all along. No one's perfect. Give me another chance," Attiq said.

"We can talk. I don't trust you. You have to gain my trust back," Anika said.

"I understand that and I will do everything I can to get your trust back, to show you I am a changed man," Attiq said.

"Well, I'll call you later. I got a call coming in from Rachel," Anika said.

"It took a long time for you to answer. Who were you talking to?" Rachel questioned.

"Attiq," Anika said.

"Attiq! You're not going to get back with him are you?" Rachel said.

"He said he's changed," Anika said.

"He hasn't changed. All he wants from you is sex!" Rachel said.

"Well, he's not getting any of that. He was hurt in his previous relationships. Once, he gave his wife a credit card to go shopping and he spent hundreds of dollars on herself and didn't bring him back anything. So he divorced her," Anika said.

"You're really smart Anika. He's just feeding you bullshit!" Rachel said.

"Everyone deserves another chance. It's not like he cheated on me or anything like that. He said he didn't know he was wrong in what he was doing," Anika said.

"You have to be smarter than that. That man doesn't love you. He's trying to use you for sex. Why can't you see that?" Rachel said.

"Well, I'm sorry for getting you involved in my relationship. Every man wants sex. He just didn't know how to go about getting it. He didn't see the value in women," Anika said.

"So you're gonna show him, huh?" Rachel said.

"I already have," Anika said. Rachel hung up the phone on Anika. She felt compelled to call Attiq back so she did.

"Do you want to ride with me to Orlando for a Muslim convention?" Attiq said.

"How long are you staying there?" Anika asked.

"For two days. I figure we get a hotel and freshen' up a bit from the long drive," Attiq said.

"When is this event?" Anika asked.

"About a month away," Attiq said.

"You just want to have sex. You know two Muslims of the opposite sex can't share a room together," Anika said.

"You've done it before," Attiq said.

"I'm not going to talk to you anymore," Anika said.

"How do you know I'm trying to use you for sex? We could have gotten two rooms," Attiq said.

"Bye Attiq. Bye," At that moment Anika realized how important Clifford was to her. She couldn't lose him. No, he wasn't as positive as she wanted him to be, but he was an honest and faithful man.

"No man is perfect," Anika thought. Anika was afraid to call Clifford. He hadn't called her in seven days. She called him a few times, but he didn't pick up the phone. Her fingers shook as she dialed his number.

"Hey. How are you doing?" Anika asked.

"I'm doing ok. I didn't hear from you so I thought you moved on," Clifford said.

"No. I thought you moved on. You didn't call," Anika said.

"Well, you were telling me how I wasn't doing right by you. You interrupted my prayer to start an argument. I'm not the enemy. I know you don't want to talk about your book, but I was just telling you that you need to get out of Saint Petersburg," Clifford said in an angry tone.

"Do you think we can have a relationship without discussing my book?" Anika questioned.

"I don't know; that book is your life. You went through blood, sweat, and tears to write it. It may be impossible not to talk about it," Clifford said.

"I think we can get through this," Anika said.

"You're still my baby aren't you?" Clifford said.

"Yes, I am. I'll call you back my mom just walked in," Anika said. "Mom, Clifford and I made up," Anika said.

"That's good honey," Ms. Muhammad said.

"It's my dream to have my man get me a publicist," Anika said.

"You can do it yourself. You don't need a man. You have to stop seeing these men as dollar signs," Ms. Muhammad said.

"It's more than just money. I wouldn't have committed myself to Clifford if he didn't have the qualities I want in a man. There's nothing wrong with wanting a man to support you financially," Anika said.

"You can do it. Get a full time job for a few months and save up the money," Ms. Muhammad said.

"I'll try." Anika grabbed the phone book and began dialing every staffing service in the book. She got hired twice and fired twice, once for dozing off at work and once for calling in sick two days in a row during her second week of employment. She was determined to get a job. So she decided to give it one more try and set up an appointment with Jennifer Staffing. They were hiring for a full time position in Palm Harbor. It was pretty far, but all Anika could see is the vision of success. When she was sick five years ago, she felt as if she was filming a movie about her life. She never knew she would write a book and a screenplay one day. She feels as if she's so close to fulfilling her dreams; so close she can taste it. Maybe Saint Petersburg wasn't feeling her, but the world would. She still had pride for her city and was determined to bring Hollywood to Saint Petersburg. She wanted to create jobs for those who are struggling, for those who had the talent, but didn't know how to show it off. She knew the importance of visualizing your success. She dreamed that the famous director, Ron Howard, would be perfect for her movie.

She wanted to end the stigma of mental illness and so did he. She met with Laura from Jennifer staffing and took a drug test. Laura handed her a script to read for the job in Palm Harbor. Laura told her to wait until 11am to call the manager. She waited for two hours and was about to call the manager when she received a phone call from Laura telling her that the manager was sick and she would have to wait a week before she could make that call.A week went by, but she didn't call the manager. She was having a hard time waking up so early in the morning and knew she would not be able to work a full time job so she started looking for an additional part-time job. Determined to get a publicist, she decided to go back to the rehabilitation center and ask for money again. This time she would have her book, press kit, and a DVD of her speech. The woman she spoke with before moved up to a manager position. She now was assigned to a young man in his early thirty's.

"Tell me what brings you in today?" Frank asked.

"I want to start my own business. Here are my press kit and my book. Every time I try to work a full time job I get fired for dozing off or missing days because of my schizophrenia and medication, but when I do a speech my anxiety attacks go away. It's like it's natural from God. I can give speeches all over the United States and charge five hundred dollars per speech. I have a BA in Psychology so I can teach the importance of taking medication. People will listen to what I have to say because I've experienced mental illness myself and I have a degree," Anika said.

"When you work full time do you have a hard time concentrating?" Frank asked.

"Yes. When I'm stressed it takes a few seconds for me to figure out what I'm supposed to do next," Anika said.

"Do you have reliable transportation?" Frank asked.

"Yes, my credit union gave me a loan for a used car," Anika said.

"You've come to us with a phenomenal idea. It will take about three months to find out if you're eligible for our services. First, you need to see a doctor, then we will meet again and I will let you know if you're eligible. You'll also need to meet with someone that handles self-employment. I'm going to set appointments for you," Frank said.

Anika didn't think first before she opened her mouth, all she could think of was getting the money for a publicist.

"Please set appointment for 11am because I need to find another job," she said. She knew then she had put her foot in her mouth and could have messed up her chances of getting a grant.

"Why do you need to get a job?" Frank asked confused.

"Because you might not be able to help me," Anika said. She realized she was negative and was shocked at what came out of her mouth. Frank still set the appointments up. He was confused, but he wanted to help. When Anika got home she checked her email and read a letter from her publisher. It said they know how to make any author a best seller. It would cost one hundred dollars to sign up, but if the plan didn't work she would be able to get her money back, so she thought she'd give it a try. She was supposed to hear back from the publisher two days after she was paid, but a week went by and she hadn't heard a word. She wrote them a letter hoping that would do the trick. Finally the publishing company wrote back.

She quickly ripped the envelope open to get to its contents, but she was quickly deflated by what she read. She was to pick a day in which to have a one day book sale, inviting all of her friends and family. It sounded like a scam. All of her family and friends had already purchased her book. She wrote the publisher asking for her money back, but they wouldn't grant her wishes. The publishing company said they had a year to turn her into a bestseller, they would not get the refund she requested. Since Anika was aware of how not listening to expert advice had negatively affected the outcome of her past efforts, she decided to revamp her thought process and do what they suggested. She would revisit the list she had of family and friends; maybe she missed a few people. And she could suggest that they purchase a copy as a gift for one of their friends. 'Brilliant', she thought. Everyone seemed excited at the idea of playing a part in what would make Anika a best- selling author so they agreed to buy a copy. She eagerly began emailing her close friends on Facebook. She needed at least five friends to send out an event notification about her one day sale. Even the celebrities she filmed agreed to help her with her quest. Anika couldn't believe it. But she didn't stop there, she let 95.7 The Beat, Tampa Bay's largest African American radio station, in on her plans. She needed them to promote her one-day sale, but her budget was small. Since she was working one job and getting disability, she thought she'd work another part-time job for a few months, just to raise the money to pay for the radio station promotion. She had a hard time finding a job that fit her schedule so she was prepared to use the little money she had saved, although she had no idea the amount it would take to produce a commercial on a radio station of this magnitude.

She dare not tell Clifford, as she knew he would not approve, but she thought it would be okay to share the information about the celebrities helping her. She excitedly called Clifford.

"Baby my publishing company thinks I can become a best-selling author. I told Soulja P about my one day sale and he said he would push it for me! I can't believe it!"

"Wow, how did you get Soulja P to agree to that?" Clifford asked.

"I filmed him before when I was a TV producer," Anika said.

"With Soulja P pushing it, you will become a best-seller. I'm going to tell my family and friends to buy your book on that day. This may work. I'm excited for you," Clifford said.Frank, from rehabilitation services, set Anika up with a doctor. The doctor asked her a few questions about her illness and had her work on a puzzle and take a psychological exam. Anika didn't understand how the doctor could diagnose her with the data he'd get from using the methods he'd chosen, but she did what he asked of her and waited for her appointment with Frank. When she arrived at Frank's office, she heard a few of the social workers talking about her.

"I don't think Frank should work with Anika, she's crazy. She will never be successful. I'm surprised she has a job," Melissa said.

"Oh trust me she won't last on her job, she's a psycho. And trying to start her own business, come on, that will never work. How can she expect to run a business if she can't keep a job? Frank told me how she tried to work full time and got fired because she was sleeping on the job. He also told me she has paranoid schizophrenia. A person like that can't be helped. She'll never make it," Dr. Smith said.

"You are so correct," Melissa said. The social workers had never even met Anika and they were unaware that she was sitting within earshot. Hearing their banter did not get Anika's hopes up about starting her own business, but when Frank called her into his office, she held her head up high.

"I got the report back from the doctor you saw and he said he is concerned about you starting your own business," Frank said.

"My mom will run the business for me. All I have to do are the speeches," Anika said.

"What if something happens to your mother?" Frank said.

"My cousin has a Master's degree in Business Administration. He would help me," Anika said. Frank had a disappointed look in his eyes like he didn't believe he could help her. He set her next appointment for the following month to give him a chance to review her psychotherapist's files. At that time she would meet with a professional who would test her to determine her ability to give speeches. She waited patiently for his call.

CHAPTER 30

All Anika wanted to do was spend time with her man. If that meant she would have to study the Bible with him, so be it. She drove over the bridge to see him after getting her hair done. When she walked in his apartment she saw the bible open on the bed. She knew he was studying hard. He went through the bible reading the words of David, Jesus, and Moses. 'Learning the bible wasn't so bad,' Anika thought. It was actually fun. She's read the bible and the Quran before, but didn't understand most of it.

"You have to decide what religion you're going to be," Clifford said.

"I will always be a Muslim. I'm not confused in any way. I know Islam is the best religion. It's just like when I asked God if there was such thing as hell and he showed me wars. I interpreted that to mean wars is like hell to God, but someone else could interpret it differently. Just focus on teaching me the bible don't try to pick my brains," Anika said.

"I want you to read John in the bible," Clifford said.

"Ok I will do that," Anika said.

"Even though you may not know the bible, you've been living your life according to the bible, and you had no idea," Clifford said.

"I do know that. I've always known. Whenever I made a mistake as a child, I would ask God for forgiveness and I never repeated those mistakes as an adult. Some people ask for forgiveness and keep making the same mistake.

A lot of people know the Bible backwards and forwards, but they are not living their life the way the bible intended. One time I was in a bible study group and we were instructed by the preacher to turn to Matthew chapter 1 and I had a hard time finding that page. A woman in the group knew that I needed help, but instead yelled out, "I know my bible!" I didn't say a word I just left never to return. That woman was probably the most sinful person of the entire group," Anika said.

"Yeah, she was probably whoring," Clifford said.

"You never know. I live every day trying to reach self-actualization. I know while I'm living on Earth I'll never be perfect because only God is perfect, but I want to come as close as I can," Anika said. Music from next door began to shake Clifford's window. He grabbed his rifle and stormed over to his neighbor's apartment. The neighbor opened the door and Clifford pointed his rifle in his face. The neighbor's eyes grew and he took a step back.

"Turn down your music or I'm going to blow your brains out," Clifford said. Clifford walked back into his house where Anika was sitting on his bed in shock.
"What did you do?" Anika questioned.

"I pointed my rifle in his face and told him to turn down the music or I'd blow his brains out," Clifford said.

"They are God's children. How could you do that?" Anika questions.

"They're still niggers. But anyway, like I was saying, even after you die you will still be learning how to become a better person. You have to learn that Jesus is the only begotten Son of God," Clifford said calmly as though the incident with his neighbor never happened.

"That's not true. Before I got sick, Jesus came to me in spirit and told me He was the Son of God. I was confused because the Quran teaches us that God cannot be begotten nor can He begot a son. I kept researching different books to find out what exactly Jesus meant when He gave me that revelation. What I've learned is Jesus called God, His father, but He didn't mean that He was the only begotten son. He meant that He was a child of God just like we all are. And Jesus did not die on the cross. He was put on the cross, but wasn't crucified. He was in a coma and His executers thought He was dead. He later married and had children," Anika said.

"Jesus came to you personally and told you He was the Son of God and you're not going to believe him?! You're going to hell!" Clifford said.

"I don't believe in a hell after death. We are living in hell on Earth. Earth is the training ground for our soul. If you believe there is a such thing as hell and then you commit an awful sin and you can't forgive yourself, you will feel like you're going to hell. And even though there is no such thing as a hell that God puts people in, your mind will conjure up a hell," Anika explained.

"I've read that some people who have had near death experiences and believed in hell, experienced going to hell in their minds. Let me tell you, the mind is powerful. If you believe in something so much your mind will make that thing true, so you have to be very careful what you chose to believe," Anika said.

"You're going to hell just like your faggot ass ex-boy-friend Mosi!" Clifford said.

"What would you say to your daughter if she came to you and told you she was gay? Would you tell her she's going to hell?" Anika said firmly. Clifford puts his head down to think clearly. There was a long pause.

"I would tell her if I was God, I wouldn't put you in hell," Clifford said. Clifford closed the bible, stormed into his room and shut the door.

Anika left Clifford's house and headed for Office Depot. She just got her hair done and she wasn't about to cover it up like some Muslims do. She had on a beautiful gray dress that covered her bosom, but showed off her arms and skin just above her chest. While she was at the counter to be served an older gentleman walked up next to her.

"I think I know you. You're someone important," Faakhir said.

"Yes, I'm an author and TV producer," Anika said. Faakhir handed Anika his business card.

"You're Muslim?" Anika asked.

"Yes, but I can see that you're not," Faakhir said.

"Yes, I am," Anika said and Faakhir burst out laughing. Anika didn't say a word. She learned from her Imam that the Quran says to dress modestly, but according to her mother when God said, 'cover thy self' he meant a woman should be a lady in public. He didn't mean she had to be covered from head to toe with clothing. That was only necessary when a Muslim prayed. Anika ignored his ignorance and walked away.

When she arrived home, she checked her mail and found another letter from her publishing company. They canceled the one day sale. Anika called her publishing company and pleaded with them not to cancel the sale, but they wouldn't budge. They had recently tried the one day sale with other authors and it did not work. Anika felt deflated. She had to tell her team of thirty people that her one day sale would not happen. She then received a call from Frank. He set an appointment up with a man that will go over her business plan and look at her speeches to see if she can make a living giving speeches. She thought her day was getting better until Clifford called.

"I don't want to see you anymore. You'll never make it as a best-selling author or a TV producer. You keep chasing this dream that will never happen. I know the statistics. If you have not made it by the time you're forty years of age, you'll never make it," Clifford said. Anika remained calm. She wasn't hurt at all. Before, she would have cursed him out, but since then she had been practicing holding her tongue. She realized that she'd already made it. Now she just has to let the world know. She knew Clifford knew nothing about being an author or a TV producer.

"Alright then it's over," Anika said. After this experience Anika decided to only date and not get serious with anyone. She didn't want to get married anyway, so why be committed. She didn't feel anything when she had sex so she felt it would be pointless to get involved with anyone. She would focus on her goals and stay away from negative people. The call Anika was waiting for finally arrived. A young lady called from the rehabilitation center to set an appointment for Anika to meet Jacob.

She had her press kit ready. Jacob was very tall and dressed in an expensive suite. First, he tested her in reading, then writing and math. Anika couldn't understand the purpose of this since she had already been speaking in the community. After the test Anika handed Jacob her press kit. He slowly went through it. She had a portable DVD player so he played the speech.

"Amazing," Jacob said. Anika lifted up her chin and grinned.

"You were meant to do this," Jacob said.

"Yes, it's a God given talent," Anika said.

"You're already doing it," Jacob said

"Yes, I am," Anika said.

"You're going to do this. You don't need us." Jacob scheduled one more meeting with Anika. This time he brought a young woman named Vicki. Anika didn't recognize her at first, but it turned out that this young lady was once Anika's rehabilitation counselor several years ago. Jacob and Vicki instructed Anika and a few other clients to work as a team and complete a project. Vicki and Jacob were really impressed by Anika's managerial and speaking skills.

"You are like night and day. I want to be there when Frank makes his decision to transfer you to the self-employment counselor. I think I have a lot to add," Vicki said.

Anika's grin stretched to her ears. She couldn't believe she just may get her funding. Now she had three people on her side. Getting the funding now should be a piece of cake. She had been called crazy by many. She had been told she'd never make it. She felt like she was so close to her dreams. Nothing can stop her now. She laid her body down to take a nap. She dreamed of getting up from her bed and reading John in the bible. Every time she tried to wake up from her dream and get the bible she was terrified. She finally awakened and headed straight for the bible given to her by one of her friends. She wondered why she was so terrified to read John in the bible. She had read a little of the bible before and it didn't bother her. She opened the bible and began to read out loud,

"Who is a liar but he that denieth that Jesus is Christ? He is the Anti-Christ that denieth the Father and the Son." She then knew exactly why she was terrified. Was Clifford right? Is Jesus the begotten Son of God?

CHAPTER 31

Anika waited for the College to call her, but they never did. She was invited to speak for the Pinellas County Urban League after one of the employees saw her flyer. Anika was very familiar with the organization. In High School they presented her with her first award; it was for an essay contest. One of the speakers at this event saw her speaking about her book and became very excited. She bought the book and brought it to the attention of a college professor. The professor enjoyed it so much that she made it required reading for her reading class. Anika could not believe she had accomplished this goal. She emailed a few professors in the past, but none of them ever responded. She wished she had someone with whom to share this good news. Her mother said someone was going to become very rich off her book and now it's coming true. Anika phoned Frank at the rehabilitation center and he called her right back and scheduled a meeting with the self-employment specialist. Anika wore her best pearls and suite she bought on credit from Ashro. She thanked God for Ashro because she didn't have enough money to buy a suite. She walked into Frank's office and saw a young woman sitting next to him. She wore her hair short and dressed in corporate wear. They both shook hands. Anika made sure her handshake was firm. She handed Malinda her press kit and book. After the formalities the meeting commenced.

"It could take anywhere from four months to three years to build a good business plan to present to rehabilitation service," Malinda said.

"Mine is going to take less than a year," Anika said.

"Is her idea feasible?" Frank asked.

"Yes, it is. I'm a little jealous. I haven't written my book yet," Malinda said.

Anika smiled. During the interview Anika's phone begins ringing. She put the phone on silent and then it started vibrating.

"You must be a popular woman," Frank said.

"Not really," Anika said with a grin on her face.

"Please look out for my email. I will email you in about a week. It was really nice meeting you," Malinda said.

Anika walked out of the building and looked down at her phone. It begins ringing again.

"Dang Anika why didn't you answer my call?" Rachel said.

"I was in a meeting to get my funding," Anika said.

"You're getting a grant?" Rachel asked.

"Yes. I'm getting funding so that I can hire a publicist to connect me to national TV and radio," Anika said.

"I bet Clifford is happy for you," Rachel said.

"I haven't told him. We broke up. He said I'm going to hell because I don't believe Jesus is the Son of God," Anika said.

"Well, he's right then. You are going to hell," Rachel said.

"I don't believe in hell. People need to be careful. If they can condemn you to hell because of something you've done wrong, then they will do the same thing to themselves. They won't forgive themselves. I try not to judge people. Why do you think there is such a thing as ghosts? Some people are afraid to go to God after they die because of the sins they've committed so they get stuck as a ghost in this world." Anika said.

"You're crazy, there's no such thing as ghosts," Rachel said.

"Just keep living. I'll call you back. Clifford is calling me," Anika said.

"I miss you," Clifford said.

"Look Clifford, I'm at the point in my life that I don't want any man right now. I'm getting my funding. I'm about to go national. I felt like I was going insane being with you. You have moments where you don't answer your phone, or you don't call me for a week. You say you're in love with me, but if that were true, you would answer my calls or return them when you're not busy?" Anika said.

"You keep chasing this dream that will never happen," Clifford said.

"My book is required reading now at Saint Pete College where I received my AA degree," Anika said. Clifford is quiet for a moment.

"You're in a different league now," Clifford said.

"I tried to tell you," Anika said.

"Let me buy you one hundred books," Clifford said.

"No, I'm moving on. I got God in my life and that's all I need. I'm not going to commit myself to anyone right now so I can focus on my book. I'm so close to becoming financially stable, I can feel it," Anika said.

"I thought I was the one," Clifford said.

"I was wrong. We should have gotten to know each other better before we committed ourselves. The things I need you to do so that I can fall in love, you won't do or don't like to do," Anika said. Clifford became silent and then hung up the phone.

Months went by and Anika didn't hear from Mosi or Clifford. She was relaxing on her couch when she heard a frantic knock at her door.

"It's 11pm, who could this be?" Anika thought. Anika looked through the peephole and saw Rachel pacing back and forth. Anika slowly opened the door.

"Wow Rachel you look good. Where have you been?" Anika questioned.

"You're not going to believe this one. I just came from Mosi's wedding," Rachel said. Anika's heart was struck with pain.

"Why didn't you tell me he was getting married?" Anika asked.

"I thought you were over him," Rachel said. Anika tried with all of her might to hold back the tears. No way was she going to cry in front of Rachel.

"Rachel you have to leave, please," Anika said. Anika shut the door and fell to her feet crying. Ms. Muhammad woke up and ran to her side.

"Honey, what's wrong?" Ms. Muhammad asked.

"Mama Mosi is married." Anika said.

"I thought you had moved on from Mosi? Ms. Muhammad said.

"No, I still dream about him all the time. I thought Clifford was the one, but I was wrong. Mosi told me he would never marry a woman unless it was me. I'm going to call him and tell him to leave her because he supposed to be with me," Anika said.

"You know people don't always stay married," Ms. Muhammad said. Anika deleted Mosi's number. She just hoped he had a Facebook so she could communicate with him. She couldn't find Mosi's Facebook, but she did find his brother's page. She opened her heart and wrote a long message.

"I cried when I found out that Mosi got married. Leaving him was the biggest mistake of my life. When you find true love stick it out through the hard times. I dated several men after Mosi and I didn't love any of them. God had already sent me my prince on a white horse. I didn't appreciate him like I should have. Don't make the same mistake I made."

Anika checked her Facebook five times a day to hope Mosi's brother would respond. A week went by and she heard nothing. Her mother checked on her every night to make sure she was ok.

"Anika I thought you told me that Mosi was gay? Why would you want to be with him?" Ms. Muhammad asked.

"He may be bisexual. I don't care about that as long as he doesn't cheat on me. So what do you think Mama? Do you think I should move on?" Anika asked. Ms. Muhammad said nothing and walked into her room to pick up her Qur'an. She had to reach, because it was the highest book on her bookshelf. She handed the book to Anika.

"Honey, you have to read the Quran. God gives us free will but in the same breath, he wants us to obey him. You must become celibate. You must learn why you keep breaking up with Mosi and then getting back with him. Your career may be growing, but your relationships are not. You have to figure out why you keep going from man to man without committing yourself to marriage. Becoming married is half your deen, as a Muslim. You have never been married. You have to question why?" Ms. Muhammad said. Anika walked back into her room with her Quran in hand. She went on Facebook and deleted the message she sent to Mosi's brother. She felt like maybe she could move on. Months went by without having dreams of Mosi. She felt like all she needed was closure. Her knowing that Mosi actually moved on helped her move on. A man was the last thing she needed at this point in her life. She committed herself to obeying God and becoming celibate. It was easy for her because most men didn't turn her on.

C HAP T E R 3 2

The phone rang and Anika answered.

"Hello, this is Glenda from Bay News 9." *'Why was Tampa Bay area's most popular television station calling her?'* she thought.

"You were selected by your community as an Everyday Hero. We'd like to interview you." Anika stood straight up. She had never been this excited in her life. When she placed the phone down, she told her mother about the call she had just received from Bay News 9. They grabbed each other and jumped up and down with joy. The same woman that referred her to the college, referred her to Bay News 9.

"This is it Mama! This is it!" Anika said. The Bay News 9 crew showed up at her house and interviewed her. Her mother didn't want to get on camera, but due to the persistence of Bay News 9's producers, she conceded. The host told Anika she should send her book and press kit to Oprah because it was very professional. The producer said the show would air in three weeks. Anika immediately posted on her Facebook, Twitter, and all of her other social media to let everyone know. This could be the break she was looking for. The interview aired a Monday. Anika watched it several times that day. It aired twelve times. The focus was on overcoming her mental illness, but not on the book so she only sold a few copies.

As a result of the show, a few people approached her inquiring about where they could buy her book. This was the most exciting thing that had ever happened to her. Raising her speaking fee now to five hundred dollars was in order, she decided. Anika called The Weekly Challenger, a newspaper in St. Pete and told her story. One of their writers promptly returned her call to schedule an interview. Anika told her she wanted to get in touch with Oprah so the reporter acquired the contact information for one of the editors at Oprah's magazine and presented it to her. Two of Anika's friends who both held master degrees and had studied marketing in college, drew up exactly what Anika needed to say to the editor. She emailed the editor and got a response back in five minutes. The editor said she would share Anika's story with her team and if they were interested they would contact her but they never did. Anika didn't believe in the devil, but sometimes she wondered if she needed to believe. As soon as she got this good news she received a phone call from Attiq.

"Hey baby how you doing? I saw you on Bay News 9. I want us to go on a date. I didn't realize how good of a woman you were," Attiq said.

"I'm not going to be in the company of a man alone. I'm celibate now. I'm trying to be obedient to God," Anika said.

"There's nothing wrong with us dating. We can date like we used to," Attiq said.

"I just told you that I'm trying to be obedient to God and you're actually trying to talk me out of it! You have a nice day," Anika yelled out. Anika had lost all hope in finding a husband. She stopped looking. She planned to have another book signing. She put an ad in one of the newspapers and they did an article on her life. She knew very little about marketing. The day arrived for her book signing. Rachel was the only one who showed up. Anika didn't realize that Rachel was growing into becoming a true friend to Anika.

"Where is everyone, Anika?" Rachel asked.

"I didn't advertise this event well enough. I know a little about marketing," Anika said.

Just as she spoke those words, one of the relatives of the store owner walked up to her table and took a seat. This man was a towering six- foot tall. He had a dark complexion and was very handsome. He wore dreads, which Anika was not attracted to.

"So you're the author my cousin was speaking so highly about? You were on Bay News 9, right? My name is Tim. How are you doing?" Tim asked.

"I'm doing fine. Only one person showed up," Anika said. "How did you market this event?" Tim asked.

"Well, I really didn't put too much into it. Like I've done before," Anika said. Tim saw a few women walking by and encouraged them to come to the table.

"Do you like to read?" Tim asked. The women blushed as Tim presented Anika's book and told her story. All three women bought a book.

"So you're good in marketing?" Anika asked.

"Yes, that's my specialty. I can help you grow your business. God's telling me to help you. There is something very special about you," Tim said.

Anika had no idea that this man would one day be her husband. She had given up on the idea of finding love.

"I'm looking for a wife," Tim said.

She wonders why this man was sharing this information with her. She remained quiet. For several months he drilled her on the proper way to give a speech, on how to find her target market, and how to perfect the look for TV. Her business plan was coming along fine. She had a meeting a few weeks away with two of the people who would decide if she was awarded the funding and a meeting with the grant writer and her counselor.

At first she had nerves, but Tim helped her learn what to say during the interview. He taught Anika about the grandness of her recounting her tale of why she wants to help save lives, how her brother died of suicide and the importance of taking medicine. She felt so calm around Tim. She thought about the possibility of dating him, but she was a Muslim and he was a Christian. He was celibate and so was she. She admired the passion he had for God because she too has such a passion. Anika was glad she made a small profit. They exchanged numbers. He was the one to call first and only after a few days had gone by. They talked on the phone for hours. Anika had always enjoyed talking on the phone with a man. She knew the subject of religion would come up soon and it did.

"How long have you been Muslim?" Tim asked. "I was born Muslim, but as an adult I said my Shahada just recently. Five years ago. I needed a place to go and worship after my breakdown. I listened to the Imam and it sounded as if he was speaking the truth," Anika said.

"What is it that your Imam does for you?" Tim asked.

"Nothing really, he bought a few of my books. When my book first came out I was excited and asked his permission to pass out flyers in his Masjid. He said yes, but one day me and my mom walked into the Masjid and he started to make a speech that sounded like he was talking about me. He said, "Don't use this Masjid to make you famous, just because you're beautiful! Get out there!" My mom and I felt that he was talking about me. I wasn't using the Masjid to make me famous, but I think that he was. He was talking about himself. When someone makes a judgment call about you and they don't know you, nine times out of ten they're talking about themselves or someone very close to them. I remained quiet. I never asked him about what he meant, but I think I should have. I haven't been to the Masjid lately. When I go I'm bored and I never learn anything that I can use to better myself. I've been going there for five years and I have only seen one person become a Muslim in front of me. I'm pretty sure other people have said their Shahada; perhaps privately with the Imam. I don't think the Masjid is growing like it should. I see the same faces. And I don't like the way some of the Muslims treat me, like when I don't have my scarf on I would speak to the woman of the Masjid but they would never speak back," Anika said.

"So why even be a part of that organization?" Tim asked.

"I was reading a spiritual book by one of the biggest psychics and she said Islam is the best religion even though she was Christian. I don't pray like the Muslims for several reasons, one of them being that I don't like wearing scarves. I get little support from the Muslims in the Masjid so I don't know why I'm a part of that organization. But I do know that Islam is a beautiful religion if you understand and interpret it correctly," Anika said. "So you say you don't pray five times a day. Do you eat pork?" Tim asked.

"Yes, a little here and there," Anika said.

"Why did you decide to say your Shahada?" Tim asked.

"Well, I was reading the Quran and it said Allah wants everyone to be Muslim. So I said my Shahada. That was the only reason why I became a Muslim. A year later I read the Quran again and I realized that the interpreter of the Quran said God wanted everyone to become Muslim not God," Anika said.

"So why are you Muslim?" Tim asked.

"Well, I guess I'm not. I'm not Muslim," Anika said. It was very difficult and painful for Anika to come to this revelation.

"I want you to read the Red letters edited by Tim J. Beals. You need to know Jesus. Imagine what you would do for the world if you knew Jesus. Why wouldn't you become Christian?" Tim asked.

"I don't believe everything in the Bible is correct. I believe some of it was changed in an effort to control the asses. That's one of the reasons God created the Quran. He promised us that none of the Quran would be changed," Anika said.

"Everything in the Bible is correct. Nothing has been changed. Why don't you come with me to my church?" Tim asked.

"I would love to do that," Anika said.

Sunday came quickly. Tim picked Anika up in his black BMW. Anika's mom peeked out of the window and smiled. She knew he was Anika's future husband. Anika was holding her book while walking up the stairs of the church and Tim's mother saw her and recognized the book.

"Weren't you on Bay News 9?" Mrs. Davis asked.

"Yes, people call me the next billionaire," Anika said.

"No, it's bigger than that," Mrs. Davis said. Anika looked up with silence. She wondered what Mrs. Davis meant. Just how famous would she be? Is it bigger than she thought? She wanted to ask what she meant, but she was scared. She walked into this massive church. You wouldn't know the church was massive at the first glance, but there was room after room connected to the church. There was a room for Sunday school, a room for editing, offices, it was really massive. This was the first time a man had taken her to church. In her mind, she thought David had taken her to church, but that wasn't real. She went to a church service on her own while she was dating Mosi. Mosi was going further and further from her mind. She stopped having feelings for him, she didn't miss him, but she didn't stop dreaming of him. She hoped that once she fell in love with a different man, the dreams would go away.

"So how did you enjoy the service today?" Tim asked.

"It was ok," Anika said.

"Did you learn anything?" Tim asked.

"I like what he said about Jesus, but I just don't see God as a punisher," Anika replied.

"How do we get punished then?" Tim asked.

"I do believe in consequences for our actions and I know what goes around comes around and some people punish us when we do wrong, but for some reason I never saw God as a Punisher. I just see him loving us unconditionally and giving us free will to learn from our mistakes and wrong doings so we can become better people." Anika said.

"You have a big heart and you will be rewarded for that," Tim said.

CHAP T E R 3 3

The time came for Anika to present her idea to the supervisor of the rehabilitation center and the former dream killer who was just recently promoted to manager. Anika was prepared and ready. Her counselor, Frank, the supervisor, Malinda who's writing her business plan, and Felisha all set in a room together. Before the interview Anika was a little nervous, but now she was calm. Felisha complimented Anika on the wonderful transformation that she has made. Malinda spoke first and briefed everyone on the importance of the meeting. The dream killer spoke next.

"Why would anyone pay you to speak?" Felisha asked.

"With all of the school shootings, people are in need of understanding why people with mental illnesses do what they do. I have been able to overcome the most debilitating mental illness known in mental health, paranoid schizophrenia. I can motivate people to live out their dreams and teach them how to overcome a mental illness," Anika said.

The supervisor was quiet, almost the entire time. Anika shared her experience on how much the average speaker makes in her industry. Everyone was impressed.

"We plan to hire a marketing person to get Anika speaking engagements. She is a good speaker, but she has no idea how to market herself and ask for a speaker's fee," Malinda said.

"Where does this person live?" Felisha asked.

"I don't know," Anika said. Malinda tried to save Anika and quickly answer their question. Anika learned a valuable lesson, not to say, "I don't know," during a meeting.

"Well, do you have the numbers from the marketing person to show how many speaking engagements she has gotten for her clients and how many books she has sold in bulk?" Malinda asked.

"I have testimonials," Malinda said.

"We need the numbers. And we need at least two more marketing persons to show us their numbers," Felisha said.

"Yes, I will have that ready for you in a week," Malinda said.

"I have to be honest. When Malinda first came to me with your plan I thought, 'Oh no, she's not going to get that,' but now I see the need," Felisha said. Malinda breathed a sigh of relief. The meeting was over and Felisha actually gave Anika a hug. Anika couldn't believe it. She actually got the dream killer on her side. Anika tried to present the Bay News 9 DVD but the portable DVD player she borrowed did not work. But Anika felt it worked in her favor because that shows she needs equipment.She left the meeting confident that she would get funding. She got in her car to go home. It was five o'clock so the traffic was heavy. The car in front of Anika stopped all of a sudden forcing Anika to put on her brakes. She tried hard to avoid running into the rear of the car in front of her, but to no avail. Her car door was jammed and the front of her car damaged. The owner of the car walked over to her immediately. Anika looked up.

"I'm so sorry. I have insurance," Anika said.

"Are you ok?" Rick asked. Another driver stumped over to Anika. Apparently he was the first to slam on his breaks.

"Is everyone ok? Do you feel any pain?" Carlos asked.

"My butt hurts," Anika said.

"Please, get out your registration and driver's license?" Carlos asked. Anika first called the police to report the accident. The representative was asking all kinds of questions so Anika got frustrated and hung up. She then phoned her job to let them know she wouldn't be able to make it in.

"Do you have your registration?" Carlos asked.

"I'm gonna get it!" Anika shouted.

"Please call the police," Rick asked.

Anika dialed the police again and answered all the questions. She then got out of the car.

"I need your telephone number," Rick said.

"Let's wait until the police gets here. Then I will see if it's ok to get give my telephone number," Anika said.

It took the police thirty minutes for them to arrive. The police had everyone move their cars. Anika made sure it was ok to give her number to the gentleman. The police authorized the exchange of phone numbers so Anika handed out her business cards.

"Wow, you're a speaker, so am I. I teach people how to think elements away. My friend had the chicken pox and I taught him how to think them away. It worked directly after he concentrated to free himself of the pox," Rick said.

"Do you have a book?" Anika asked.

"No, but I'm working on it," Rick said.

The officer talked to Rick and Carlos alone and then went over to Anika. She gave Anika a ticket for reckless driving even though there was bad traffic. Anika was pissed, but that's what she expected from the police. She gave Tim a call and to cheer her up, he picked her up and drove her to a beach. They sat in front of the sun and watched the sunset while sipping on white wine and eating cheese. Anika's body felt so relaxed. She thought that maybe wine is what she needed to relax her so the next day she bought a bottle and enjoyed one glass. She didn't feel relaxed at all. She felt nothing but drunk. The following day Tim told her she was snapping at people. She knew it was because of the wine. Tim told her that the only reason she was relaxed with him was because of the romance. Anika knew she could easily become an alcoholic because her father was one. And she knew the warning signs of addiction from her Psychology courses. The next day the FL Sentinel arrived. She had subscribed to this newspaper because it connects her to the community. It helps her connect with people for speaking engagements. She read an article about the Tampa Bay Black Journalist Association coming to her job to do an event. She knew she would miss it because of not having a car so she emailed the coordinator for the event. Anika talked about how she was awarded for being an Everyday Hero in her community and about overcoming paranoid schizo-phrenia. The coordinator referred the email to the president of the association and the next day she emailed Anika. She said she wanted to interview her and put her in two-hundred differ-ent newspapers and magazines, some being National.

As soon as Anika's mother walked in the house Anika ran up to her to tell her the good news.

"This is it Mama! This is it! The president of the Tampa Bay Black Journalist Association wants to interview me and she's going to make me national!" Anika said.

"It is never it. Life is a journey and as long as you have a dream and you're working towards that goal you're on a journey that will continue. And as long as you stay on your path, you are already successful. It is never it; you can always be better. Don't think of the journey. Keep your mind focused on the goal. That's why some people don't reach their dreams because they're too busy concentrating on the journey," Ms. Muhammad said.

"I guess that's why I'm so successful because I love the journey. I don't know how I'm going to get home from work since I don't have a car," Anika said.

"Don't worry about it honey, I'll pick you up from work," Ms. Muhammad said. The next day Anika started her long journey to catch the bus on to work. It was so hot that day. She was sweating profusely. She prayed to God for some relief; for it to rain on her and that next second, rain started to fall.

"Thank you God," Anika said. It was only raining on her. The area away from her was dry. Anika got on one bus, then another, then another. It took her three hours to get to work and she became so stressed but she arrived early. She called up Tim to help relieve her stress. He then invited her to get a professional massage with him. Anika's phone begins to ring. Anika asked Tim to hold and she clicks over.

"Hey Anika you got fifty dollars I can borrow? I need some gas," Rachel said.

"Sure," Anika said.

"I'll call you back I'm on the phone with Tim," Anika said.

"Wait! You won't believe this! Mosi's wife is pregnant," Rachel said.

"Rachel please don't tell me anything else about Mosi. I'm over him," Anika said.

"Ok, I just thought you should know," Rachel said. Anika clicks over back to Tim.

"That was Rachel, I'm so sick of her. She wants to borrow money, but she annoys me talking about Mosi. I'm not going to let her borrow a dime," Anika said.

"Do you have the money?" Tim asked.

"Yes," Anika said.

"You have to show her love even though she is negative. God will bless you for that," Tim says. Three weeks of taking the bus to work went by but it was ok because Anika absolutely loves her job. She doesn't like working, but she likes the people she meets at work and the way the job is structured. She loves to attend their groups. They have a Pride group, African American group, Asian group, and a group for the disabled. They offer a Toastmasters class that they pay for and Anika has taken full advantage of these classes.

A few of her co-workers have seen her on Bay News 9. Her team lead posted the Bay News 9 video on the screen for the entire call center to see. If Anika had worked for any other company she would not have revealed that she had an illness, but with this company she felt comfortable. One of the co-workers told her that she felt she could do anything she put her mind to after seeing the Bay News 9 video. She had a lesser disability and now looked up to Anika. One of her encouraging co-workers named Alex walked up to her as she was clocking out to go home.

"So what happened with your story that was supposed to go National?" Alex asked.

"It made the paper, but it didn't go National. I have to keep pushing. It will happen one day," Anika said.

CHAPTER 34

Two months went by and Anika was ready to present her case to the rehabilitation center. This was the final meeting. Anika wasn't nervous at all; Malinda prepared her well. Frank, the supervisor, and Malinda made it to the final meeting, but Felisha, the dream killer, did not make it because she was sick. Anika handed everyone a copy of the business plan that she had pre-pared. Malinda started the meeting,

"I recommend Anika for self-employment with finan-cial support provided by the rehabilitation center based on the business plan in the amount of one million. This is not my plan; this is the business plan that will showcase Anika's needs for her business. Anika has been very timely and thorough in her research. She has been able to make difficult concrete deci-sions after analyzing the data and receiving counsel and she has experience in the field. It is the opinion of CBTAC, The Certified Business Technical Assistance Consultant, that that Ms. Muham-mad will be a successful business owner. Anika go ahead and go over your startup needs for your business."
Anika stood and prepared to tell her story.

"I was diagnosed with the most debilitating mental illness known in mental health, paranoid schizophrenia. Coun-selors with master degrees said I was crazy, would never find a job and would never find a job and should be stuck in a mental institution for the rest of my life. I've maintained a job now for many months and I'm a Bay News 9 Everyday Hero. Malinda, please show the clip." Anika said. Everyone watched with their mouths open.

"That was amazing," the supervisor said.

"Turn to page four. I will be selling my speeches on, "Living Out Your Dreams Regardless of Your Disability," I will be selling my book and motivational DVD. I will begin to speak locally and then nationally. I've learned you have to be famous in your city first before you go national. My target market is mental health non-profits, churches, colleges, and high schools. My industry is growing, especially in the areas of motivational and self-help. Leonor McCall-Rodriguez states, "Having been in this industry for years, I can share that the market downturn has brought a revitalization of the motivational speaking career as people seek new focus, pursue change, and push forward." Not only do I have a BA in Psychology, I also have first-hand experience with mental illness. Having been diagnosed with Paranoid Schizophrenia, I am able to motivate others through my own experience. Using the latest and best computers and software, I will not only be able to write my speeches, I will be able to lay out books to upload onto the self- publishing website and see it to fruition, creating a quality product." Anika said.

"Many authors starting out are not able to afford quality marketing materials. With family support, as well as requested support from the rehabilitation office, I will have quality marketing materials at start up. With training provided by the National Speakers Association Academy, I will be able to promote myself and acquire paid speaking engagements." Anika said.

Anika's presentation of her business plan was so good that the supervisor approved her funding on the spot; all of one million dollars. Anika wanted to give the news to the most important person in her life, her mom. She called her mother and Tim over to her house to give the good news. It had been several months and Anika no longer had dreams about Mosi. She was completely over him. She did not miss him in any way. She pulled up to her house at the same time as Tim and her mother were driving up.

"Mama, Tim, I got my funding," Anika said. Anika's mother grabbed her and hugged her and they both started jumping up and down once again. Then Tim gave her a hug and told her congratulations. He then takes her by the hand and walks her into her room and shuts the door.

"Anika I'm a disciple of Jesus. I believe that Jesus is the begotten Son of God. I want to make sure when you come in front of the world you reveal the truth. I want you to teach what God has taught you. I'm able to hear God at times," Tim said.

"Well, Jesus did come to me in my sleep and told me he was the Son of God but the Quran says differently. What would you do if you were raised as Muslims, but your revelations shows Christians may be right about God and Muslims wrong? What would you do?" Anika asked.

"Anytime you get a revelation from God you're supposed to ask God to reveal the meaning of your revelations. When you lay for sleep tonight I want you to ask God if Jesus is the begotten Son of God," Tim said.

"I also asked God if there was such thing as hell and he took me to a different planet where wars were taking place. The answers He gave me were confusing. I think I misinterpreted them," Anika said.

"Hell does exist," Tim said.

"Well, do you believe that God puts people in hell?" Anika asked.

"Would you let a stranger live in your home?"

"No," Anika said.

"God cannot let anyone in his home without the right key. Everyone on the team with the Lord is a part of his house," Tim said.

"Your language dictates what you call that other home. Some say hell others say a dark place and some say it's a place that is absent of God's grace and mercy, where his love is not experienced. No matter how you label it, it's not what I want for me or those that I love. In other words, I want them to have the right key to get in his house," Tim continued.

"You didn't answer the question. Does God put people in hell?" Anika asked.

"The answer would be yes and no. It's like choosing a car. Say you pick the blue car and I say go forth and get in that blue car. Did I put you in that blue car or did you choose to be in that blue car? It's the same with heaven. If you choose to go to heaven, which belongs to God, you must choose to receive the path that he has for you to get there. And the only path to the kingdom is through the kingdom and that path is Christ." Tim said.

Silence enters the room. That night, Anika asked God if Jesus was the begotten Son of God. She envisioned God speaking to her through Tim. She couldn't remember what Tim was saying in the dream, but she did remember Tim speaking God's words. She couldn't believe the Christians were right about Jesus. Tim came to visit her the next day and she asked him what she had to do to get saved. He looked in her eyes and said, "To be saved you have to ask Jesus to be the Lord of your life and let Him be the Lord of your life." Then he asked her, "Do you want Jesus to be the Lord of your life?"

"Yes, I do," Anika said.

Then he said, "Repeat after me. Lord Jesus come into my life and be my King. Rule over me and enter my life. Be my Savior and save me.Come into my life, be my master and master me. I submit to you and I ask you to remake me in your image as king, as savior, and as my master. I believe that you died on the cross Lord for my sins and that you were raised from the dead so that I may have eternal life. In the mighty name of Jesus, Amen." Just as Anika said those few words she received a call from one of her good friends. She wanted her to fly out to the University to give a paid speech. Anika begins traveling all over the nation. She had made it. She had been saved. It was a dream fulfilled.

Don't Call Me Crazy! is fiction but inspired by my true story. Learn what parts are similar and how I strived despite schizophrenia. If you want to grab this short story, claim your copy when you join my newsletter.

Visit www.swiyyah.com

To God be the glory.

Thank you mom for believing in me and teaching me that life is 1% what happens to you and 99% how you react to it.

Special thanks to my mom, Halimah Kencler, who has believed in my dreams and encouraged me to never give up; to my loving husband, Dederick Woodard, who loves me like no man has ever loved me and helps me to sustain my business. Thank you to my wonderful business consultant, Yolanda Cowart, who is one of the people responsible for the success of my business. Thanks to Emad, Maurice, Monique, Alim Muhammad, Faheemah Muhammad, Yakyah Muhammad, Lateefah Haugabrook, Ibn Abdullah, Steve Manning of SMS Excellence, Tia Grant, Wayne Brass Usf, Rashida Strober of play "A Dark Skinned Woman's Revenge," Jerry Coleman, Feven Hunde, James Evans, Candy Lowe of Candy Lowe Tea Time Tampa, FL, and my loving family and friends.

Thank you for reading Don't Call Me Crazy! I'm Just in Love. Your honest review will help future readers decide if they want to take a chance on a new-to-them author.

About the author

Swiyyah Nadirah Woodard was born in the housing projects of Saint Petersburg, FL. Her father left when she was three so she was raised in a single parent home. At the age of five she was molested by her eight year old brother. She later started school. She had slurred speech and didn't care to make friends so she was bullied by her peers. At the age of eight, she wanted to kill herself because a girl wanted to fight her. She looked in the medicine cabinet for medication. Thank God, she couldn't find any.

As a teenager she was physically abused by her step dad. The abuse was so severe, God blocked it from her memory. At the age of 20 the brother that molested her committed suicide, which was devastating to her and the entire family. Swiyyah has always viewed herself as normal. She never received any disciplinary problems in school, made good grades, and received her BA degree in Psychology from the University of South Florida.

When the doctors diagnosed her with the most debilitating mental disorder known in mental health, paranoid schizophrenia, she denied it. She questioned their expertise. She refused to take medication. She was then hospitalized six times. Her family took a picture of her at her worst and that's when she knew she needed help. She has been taking medication now for six years without a relapse.

She is now a published author and a National Motivational Speaker. Her first book is entitled, "Don't Call Me Crazy! I'm just in Love," and is inspired by her true story. It is now required reading for SPC College.

Because of her experiences, she has grown closer to God and has learned a lot about life, much of which she reveals in her speeches. Swiyyah has done extensive research, shares her personal experiences, and provides the warning signs she exhibited as a child. She provides resources to help the community and teaches them how to live out their dreams regardless of their disability. Swiyyah was selected as Bay News 9 Everyday Hero, which was seen by two million viewers.

Please contact Swiyyah to book speaking engagements, radio and TV interviews, or to purchase a book at www.dontcallmecrazy.com.

Find Swiyyah on social media.

https://www.bookbub.com/authors/swiyyah-woodard
www.facebook.com/dontcallmecrazy
www.instagram.com/dontcallmecrazyimjustinlove
www.twitter.com/swiyyah
www.linkedin.com/in/dontcallmecrazyimjustinlove

Made in the USA
Middletown, DE
02 May 2024

53785095R00142